leave
me a review. Thank
Jill Griffin

Who Says? & other Short Stories

JILL GRIFFIN

Produced by TN Traynor Publishing

First Printed Edition, England November 2024

ISBN: 9798301286605

Contents

Book Description

WHO SAYS & OTHER SHORT STORIES — JILL GRIFFIN

Life is a patchwork quilt of laughter, heartbreak, and the unexpected—and Jill has stitched together a collection of tales and poems that celebrate all its glorious contradictions.

From poignant reflections on love and loss to laugh-out-loud memories and made-up mischief, this compilation offers a little something for everyone. If you've ever laughed with Alan Bennett's *Talking Heads,* marvelled at the quirky charm of Nora Ephron's *I Feel Bad About My Neck,* or cherished the tender whimsy of Joanna Cannon's *The Trouble with Goats and Sheep,* you'll find a kindred spirit in Jill's work.

Perfect for fans of uplifting reads and bittersweet chuckles, Who Says? & Other Short Stories is a delightful escape into a world where truth mingles with imagination, and every page brings a fresh surprise.

Inside, you'll find memoir snippets that stir the soul, short stories that make you giggle or gasp, and poems that dance between wit and wonder.

Take a seat, pour a cuppa, and dive into Jill's world—you won't want to leave.

Dedication

To Rob, my greatest fan.

Thanks go to my editor, Tracy.

Wanderer's Delight

From mountain peaks to ocean shores,
Jill wanders wide, the world explores.
With a cheerful heart, a spark in her eye,
She dances beneath each changing sky.

Through bustling streets and quiet lanes,
In sunlit fields and misty rains,
She finds the magic, near and far,
Each journey's path her guiding star.

In tales she weaves and stories told,
Her spirit shines, both brave and bold.
For every step, a memory is made,
In poems and prose, her travels laid.

So open these pages, come along,
To lands of laughter, light, and song.
Where Jill's adventures bloom and thrive,
And words of wonder come alive.

Chaos, it's the New Cocaine!

MOVING TO THE GRADE II listed corn mill by the ford was everything we'd dreamed of. A little surreal, with its quaint front and quirky features. The mill offered the perfect balance: a quiet, semi-rural retreat, yet just a walk from the nearest town. We couldn't have been happier.

From the mill, the view stretched across green, rolling hills, framed by the soft sounds of the River Blythe just a stone's throw away. A wooden footbridge crossed the nearby ford, with a gauge rising up to six feet. Good for motorists, we thought, though the idea of the water ever reaching that height seemed laughable.

The property boasted a four-acre forest, plus a fenced area marked for its 'historical interest and natural beauty.' It was a magnet for visitors, who were captivated by the remnants of the old mill machinery. The grand wheel, still proudly resting by the mill's side, seemed almost alive, as though a flick of a switch could set it spinning again. The Machinery Floor, with its wooden aroma and rustic charm, had been transformed by a glass floor, making it a favourite spot for reading or dreaming up novels. A bygone era cast its spell of make-believe and my imagination soared.

On any given day, children played by the ford, and cars rumbled through the shallow water. From the bedroom window, I often watched the scene below. Though anglers were few and far between, a plethora of fish swam in the river.

We'd done our due diligence: checked local plans, reviewed the flood defence system put in by the owners nineteen years before, and asked every possible question. With home insurance sorted and a bargain price paid, life at the mill became idyllic.

Years before, I'd once joked about wanting to try a 'space cake' in Amsterdam—to experience that fabled high. Of course, I'd never wanted to take anything too strong—Catholic guilt wouldn't allow it. Now, the mill gave me that thrill. It was perfect: peaceful, yet close enough to Solihull to indulge in a bit of shopping whenever I pleased.

Then came a January day that changed everything. After eight months in the mill, we'd made friends, joined the local History Society—an obvious step for mill owners—and settled into the rhythm of life here. The morning rain started as a drizzle, drawing children out to splash by the ford, umbrellas bobbing alongside their laughter. Even our youngest, Lucy, joined the fun, and I captured the moment with my camera. A perfect moment, I thought with a smile.

Rob glanced at his phone. "Says 100% rain later—starting around two. Think we should put the flood defence gate in, just in case?"

There was a small two-foot wall in front of our house with a sturdy wooden gate which led to our front door, surely that would keep our home safe for now? "We're fine," I replied. "The ford's only a foot deep, and it's a fair distance from the mill. Let's wait and see; forecasts are often wrong."

"Alright," he said, "but I'll check the pumps, especially the one on the ford side."

By afternoon, the rain had intensified. From the window, I spotted an Uber, stranded mid-ford. Its driver perched on the roof, his voice cutting through the downpour. "HELP, ANYONE, I can't move my car!"

The water had risen to four feet and was inching toward us.

"Rob, we're needed outside. I'll call the fire brigade. Let's get the flood defence gate in, too."

Outside, the waterline was climbing. The Uber driver, unable to swim and panicked, refused to climb down, while the owner of a Range Rover stood by trying to help. I could see Rob wrestling the floodgate into place, and he called out, "They're on the way—five minutes out!"

'Nee-naw. Nee-naw.' The fire engine siren offered me a sense of calm, help was on the way. I could only think of one thing needed in a crisis—tea. As I entered the mill to make refreshments, I expected to hear at least one of the three pumps in action. Instead of the reassuring humming of an engine, the trickle of water seeping under the mill door mocked me.

"Oh God, it hasn't activated, Rob! Water's getting in!"

He rushed to the control panel. Dead. The main switch had failed. With growing urgency, he dialled Fred, the local engineer.

"Fred, we need your help, please. The pumps aren't working. Water's coming in fast. The ford is nearly six feet deep."

Fred's voice was calm. "Try flipping the mains supply off and on."

No luck. By now, the kids were in tears, but at least the Uber driver was back on solid ground. Thunder rumbled as sheets of rain battered the landscape. Fred was already on his way, but the mill seemed defenceless.

Rob's face was white. "It's not worked."

"I'm on my way," said Fred.

Sitting on the front wall, tea in hand, we spoke to the fire brigade as they placed sandbags around the mill and put 'stop' signs up to prevent further traffic from attempting to cross.

When Fred appeared, tools in hand, we all cheered. Like a trooper, he's had to park a way off and walk the rest of the way. He went straight to the control panel and began his magic with the soldering iron. Within minutes, the pumps roared to life, humming through the walls. The water was the highest Fred had ever seen and he worked at breakneck speed, and soon the worst was behind us.

Though the floors needed a thorough clean, we knew we'd managed to avoid any lasting damage. By nightfall, we'd opened the windows to air out the damp, our ordeal nearly over.

Fred spent the night to keep an eye on the pumps, we promised him a flow of beer which he accepted knowing we had ploughed all our funds into restoring the mill and had nothing left for a rainy day!

Exhausted, we took stock. The flood had brought us to our knees, but with grit and a bit of luck, we'd pulled through. We'd had a day of despair and panic laced with an incredible adrenaline rush. With determination and many helpers, we had saved our mill and rescued the Uber driver.

Life here might be unpredictable, with highs and lows sharper than any drug. Why bother with a space cake?

Chaos, it's the new cocaine!

Fowl Stories!

BUYING A RUN-DOWN chicken farm hadn't even crossed my mind, but here we were. I couldn't help but wonder—would I regret it?

When my dad visited the farm with me, he frowned at the empty coops and sprawling land. "I don't get it," he said. "You've got a nice house already. Why take on all this work?"

Part of me wanted to agree. It was a massive undertaking. But I replied, "It's a project. We could keep some chickens, maybe geese too. The house repairs would keep us busy for years."

Settling in, we bought six Rhode Island Red chickens, each one identical to the next. We called them all Betsy. They clucked around, scratching at the earth, settling into their coop at nightfall. They were cheerful little creatures, rewarding us daily with fresh eggs, like small gifts each morning.

Betsy in the Spotlight!

One day, we got an unexpected call from the Concordia Theatre. They needed a chicken for a play. Her role would be simple: a nightly appearance, being carried across the stage. No singing or dancing or quacking jokes. We'd stay and watch every show, and take her home to bask in her glow.

We chose our boldest Betsy, marking her leg with a small ring to tell her apart. That first night, she trembled in the actor's arms, but by the end of the week, she had settled into her new role, clucking to the audience, who couldn't get enough. After a standing ovation one night, the director asked, "Could Betsy join the encore? And perhaps the after-show party?"

Of course, we said yes. Betsy enjoyed her parties, too. She'd stroll about the cast, pecking and clucking as they doted on her.

When she returned to the coop, though, something had changed. Unlike before, when she would huddle up with the others, the ringed Betsy now roosted by herself, on the other side of the coop. She'd become a star—determined, it seemed, to remind the others of her new status. Even now, long after her stage debut, she's still a 'diva' in her own right and still wearing the ring around her leg. Sometimes I expect her to offer me her ankle to kiss her mark of distinction. With regular visits from the cast, her status is held in place.

Desmond Joins the Flock

One day, we received a warm duck egg as an unusual trade for four of our own chicken eggs. What to do with it? Fry it? Make a cake? Or let one of the Betsys hatch it?

We tucked the duck egg under our most broody Betsy. She didn't seem to notice the larger egg, settling over it with her usual maternal focus. Weeks later, she proudly hatched a fluffy white Aylesbury duckling, complete with bright orange legs and beak. We named him Desmond, though we couldn't say why.

Our broody Betsy didn't notice Desmond's waddle or his love of puddles, nor bat an eye at his bill and webbed feet. She fussed over him like he was the fluffiest chick in the coop.

Desmond took to the chickens as if he were one of them, scratching around and even popping inside the kitchen for treats. At night, while the Betsys roosted on the perch, Desmond would nestle on the coop floor nearby. He seemed perfectly content, but I sometimes wondered if he missed the water. And he was the only duck around which delivered waves of guilt.

Thinking he might like company, we brought home Jemima, another Aylesbury. As soon as she saw Desmond, she rushed toward him. He looked at her in horror—she was nothing like his chicken family. Desmond fled, racing around the garden, desperate to escape this weird creature. Jemima, though, wouldn't be left behind. She quacked and flapped, determined to be by his side.

I stood back, utterly gobsmacked—I'd imagined they'd click instantly, but Desmond looked at Jemima as if she'd just landed from Mars! Should she try her luck again? Would she get through to him? Jemima was on a mission alright, waddling toward Desmond with single-minded determination and hissing at any feathered or furry creature that dared block her path!

It went on for hours until Desmond, with wings drooping like wilted leaves and a wobble in his step, flopped to the ground in utter defeat as dusk rolled in. Jemima sat beside him, their beaks barely touching in a sort of truce. Soon enough, they were inseparable, waddling to the kitchen together each morning. It seemed life had returned to normal—until one night, they stayed out too late.

In the dark, a fox struck, but Desmond defended Jemima valiantly, fighting the vixen off with everything he had. He injured his leg in the process, and I feared the worst. With a heavy heart, I took him to the vet. The leg was broken beyond repair, the vet explained, and Desmond would limp from then on. "He won't be able to fend off a fox again," the vet warned.

But life without Desmond wasn't an option. I paid for the treatment and took him home, hoping for the best.

Back at the farm, Jemima and the Betsys waited anxiously. When Desmond waddled out of his cardboard box, they gathered around, clucking and quacking. Desmond had returned—a hero among his friends. It was the best forty pounds I ever spent!

Oddly enough, I later broke out in red spots. The doctor said it was an allergy to duck feathers, of all things. I laughed, saying, "That's quackers!" Still, Desmond stayed.

In time, we added a new member to our little flock—a honking, hissing goose named Gregory. Now that was a feathered friend I was allergic to—but that's another story.

So, was buying the farm a mistake? Not at all. It's a feathered, chaotic life, but I wouldn't change a thing.

Living the Dream

GROWING UP WITH adoring parents, I had a childhood most would envy. I was their 'everything,' and they made sure I knew it. The only thing I ever longed for but never got was a sibling—someone to play with, to share secrets with, to be my friend. As a young child, I endlessly asked for a baby brother or sister. Every time I brought it up, Mum's face flushed a deep red as she stared at the floor, avoiding Dad's wistful glances. His face would crumble, his rich brown eyes dimming, and he'd start pacing the room, a silent frustration settling over him.

The tension would hang in the air until I couldn't take it anymore, and I'd rush to him, planting a kiss on his cheek, knowing he needed it.

With a smile as bright as a lighthouse beam, he'd say, "You're our angel, Lucy. We couldn't have wished for a more perfect child, could we, Love?"

In her tailored twin-set and smart skirt covered with a fresh apron, Mum pretended to dust the table, her fingers trembling as she adjusted a perfectly aligned framed photo of the three of us. Her wavy brown hair always fell softly around her freckled face, but in moments like this, her deep blue eyes clouded with something hidden, a sorrow she never voiced. "Lucy, you're all we've ever wanted or needed. Now, let's have a group hug."

Her voice was always soft yet firm, a practised poise that came from years of managing emotions she kept locked away. She would smile brightly, but in those moments discussing more children, light never reached her eyes. When she hugged me, a faint scent of Estée Lauder filled my nose. And beneath the polished exterior was a woman who worried about everyone but herself.

We'd laugh, clinging to one another, happy to have dodged the painful topic once again. In time, it became a no-go area, and a few months after the last of these discussions, I got the best gift ever—Rufus, my faithful dog. He followed me everywhere, shared all my secrets, and completed our little family.

Maybe it was because I was an only child, but I grew up a little spoiled and a lot independent. I didn't share my toys, clothes, or time with others. I was old beyond my years, preferring books to people, and I never fitted in with other kids, with the exception of my best friend, Alice. I wasn't invited to parties, and I spent my school breaks reading in a quiet corner. Alice, shy and sweet, totally got me. She was my only ray of sunshine in a grey world.

My parents saw only the best in me, of course. They always did. I learned how to wrap them around my finger.

Mum would always say, "You deserve the best, Darling. Don't settle for less," as she tidied the house, her fingers brushing against the small tattoo of me. She'd cover it with makeup whenever she dressed up for an evening out, but it was always there—a mark of devotion on her leg that she never let anyone see.

To the outside world, I had it all. Anything I wanted, I got. Mum and Dad always said yes.

Then one day, Alice shunned me in the playground, hooking her arm through an older girl's and skipping away. The last grip

I had on life began to slip. Alone and adrift, I didn't seem to belong—neither with my family nor my peers. That's when the bulimia started. It gave me control, made me believe I was strong in at least one part of my life.

So why did I hate myself? Why did I have this constant need to rebel?

I was given everything—love, comfort, a future anyone would dream of. But instead of being grateful, a hollow space grew within me, restless and unfulfilled. Like I was chasing something no one else could see. Maybe that's why I pushed against it all, the perfect life they had built for me. I couldn't stand the pressure of being their perfect little girl. Maybe if I broke myself down first, no one else could.

By sixteen, I was skinny, a loner, and desperate to break free from the suffocating love of my parents. They worshipped me, placed me on a pedestal, but I needed to be someone different to what they wanted. I craved the rebellion they would never understand.

That's when I became a Goth. Black became my uniform—silk, velvet, leather, PVC, you name it. Occasionally, I'd throw on a splash of bold colour, but it was always dramatic, always meant to stand out. My soft-brown waves were dyed jet black, a transformation as sharp as my attitude. My freckles vanished beneath layers of thick foundation. A black septum ring gleamed, deep red lipstick made my lips unmissable, while dark eyeliner framed my blue eyes in a way that demanded attention. For the first time, I felt truly visible.

My voice was my ticket to a new world. I sang in the school choir, and my talent earned me an invitation into a group of like-minded creatives. We met every day at a disused railway station in Lapworth. I became the lead singer for their band, Black Maria, alongside Jeff. He was older and mysterious, and I was soon hopelessly in love.

Jeff was twenty-two, wry and self-deprecating, with wild black hair, smeared lipstick, and smudged eyeliner that gave him an untouchable edge. His raspy voice and guitar skills made him unobtainable, way out of my league, but somehow, he saw something in me no one else did. And that was all that mattered.

Mum and Dad, of course, didn't approve. They despised the new me and my new boyfriend even more. One of the milder things they said was—"he needs a good wash."

I started coming home later and later. Eventually, I decided not to return at all. I stayed with Jeff at the station, sleeping rough among the graffiti-covered walls and piles of discarded spray cans. The place was a shrine to decades of youth culture, and I was in awe of it—the decay, the history, the freedom.

That became my life for the next six months.

My grades plummeted and with it my dreams of getting into a good university drifted further and further away. Mum and Dad begged me to come home.

"It's too cold for you to sleep rough," Mum pleaded. "Tell her, Patrick."

Dad nodded. "Your mum's right. Come back. You can bring Jeff if you want."

Mum's lips curled as she gave Dad a hostile glare.

I pouted. "She doesn't want him to come."

Dad glared at Mum, his hand balled into fists, his jaw tight. "Of course, Jeff's welcome."

Through gritted teeth, Mum forced a smile. "Yes, of course. Jeff can stay."

For a couple of weeks, we behaved. Jeff helped out around the house, mowing the lawn and pulling weeds, while I buried myself in my studies, pretending everything was normal. The garden was immaculate—straight lines, blooming roses—but inside, I was falling apart.

The bulimia crept back in, driven by that need for control. Beneath the surface, nothing felt right. My world was tilting, the ground shifting beneath me. I knew it wouldn't be long before everything spun out of control, leaving me tumbling through the chaos.

Always stoic, Mum hid her worry. "It's so good to have you home."

Dad agreed with a nod. "Yes, it's been far too long."

They were blind to the cracks forming beneath the surface.

Every day, Jeff would disappear for his walk back to the station, always growing more distant, more secretive. His excuse—he needed to see his friends. His eyes were bloodshot, his nose constantly running. I knew what was happening, but I tried to ignore it. Mum, of course, thought it was just hay fever.

I started skipping classes to accompany Jeff back to the station. I missed the place, the freedom it offered. But things had changed since we'd moved out. Wildflowers in jam jars now decorated every room, the smashed windows were repaired, and the sun streamed in, casting everything in a warm, golden glow.

Today as we strode along the deserted platform to the station house, a shiver ran down my back that had nothing to do with the autumn breeze. A premonition, maybe, that everything was about to change. Worried, I slipped my hand into Jeff's as we entered the building.

Then I saw her—a vision in a flowing pink dress. The kind that clung to her in the breeze, swirling around her legs like a dancer caught in motion. Her long, unkempt blonde hair was strewn with tiny wildflowers, giving her an ethereal, otherworldly air. Bracelets jangled on her wrists, layered with leather straps and woven beads as if she'd raided a festival stall.

She glided into the room, barefoot, radiating a carefree confidence that irritated me more than prickly heat. The thick scent of patchouli and incense followed her, overwhelming and cloying, hanging in the air like a statement. She walked straight up to Jeff, kissed him, and staked her claim. Her eyes told me everything—she wasn't just passing through.

Jeff stepped back with an awkward shrug. "Becky, this is Lucy. The girl I told you about. I'm staying with her parents."

My mind raced. Where had I seen her before?

She smiled, but her eyes were cold. "She's not what I expected."

I stiffened, a wave of anger washed over me.

Jeff let go of my hand. Shoving his in his pockets, he shared a secret smile with the detestable hippy.

I rushed outside, bile rising in my throat. As I heaved into the makeshift toilet, Becky's laughter echoed behind me, cruel and mocking.

I wiped my face, forcing myself to breathe. I won't let her take him. One thing's for sure—the hippy and I are never going to be friends. Quietly, I tiptoed to the window and watched them share a spliff, passing it back and forth, their heads close together, whispering God knows what. Tiny pricks of tears stung my eyes, but I gritted my teeth and refused to give them the satisfaction of seeing me upset.

When I stepped back into the room, I heard her whisper to Jeff, "I have a surprise for you later. Come back alone."

Jeff stubbed out the spliff they were sharing, grinding it into the floor. "You alright, Babe? You rushed out, and I wasn't sure if I should've come after you to check."

"Just a banging headache. Felt sick, that's all. I'm better now."

I slipped my arm around his waist, relieved for Becky's overpowering incense smell as it would cover any unpleasant smell that might be around me. "Let's go home. Leave Becky to carry on sprucing up the place."

I gave her a cold, dismissive look, up and down. "It looks… fabulous. You lot must be so proud. We'll come back soon to see how you're getting on. Will you still be here?"

Becky folded her arms, but Jeff shot her a look, silently warning her to keep quiet.

I dragged him outside, slamming the door behind us. One up for me.

We walked in silence, each wrapped in our own thoughts. I didn't trust Jeff, but I couldn't blame him entirely—I didn't expect anyone to treat me well. I thought about Becky. There was something about her—something familiar. She was full of life, colourful and natural, with a kind of wild, untouchable beauty. She reminded me of a girl I knew at school. But that Becky had dark hair and a darker mood, it couldn't be her.

"Race you to the park!" I tapped Jeff on the arm before sprinting ahead.

Jeff's lithe frame powered past me, his elbow catching me as we reached the tree. We tumbled onto the grassy bank and made love in a secluded spot, tangled in each other. For a moment, bliss swept through me. I was the girl he adored, still his Goth, wrapped up in the silent music of us.

Afterwards, basking in a shared glow, I smiled, almost… at peace.

"I need a smoke."

"But you quit, you haven't touched one for months. Though you had one with Becky earlier…"

"Not cigarettes. A spliff." His voice sharpened. "Don't give me that look. Don't go all holier-than-thou on me."

"I'm not." I got up from the grass. "But we agreed, no spliffs, especially at my parents' house."

"Spliffs are nothing. Just a bit of weed. I used to inject worse, and you did too if I remember right." His eyes narrowed, and he sneered, disgust clear in his voice. "You're such a bloody goody two-shoes these days."

Heart racing, my hands trembling, I took a step back. "But you promised..."

I didn't see it coming. His fist slammed into me, knocking me down. I hit the ground hard as the kicks followed, one after another, raining over my body. Curled up, shielding myself, each breath came in shallow gasps, my chest tight with fear. Panic gripped me so hard that I had to fight to keep air in my lungs. Each new pain shocked my mind as well as my body.

"Get up, you crazy bitch!" he snarled, standing over me. "You deserved that. Stop crying or I'll head straight back to the station."

Through swollen eyes, I glanced around the park. Kids were playing in the distance, oblivious. My body ached, bruises already forming in deep purple patches. Blood trickled down my chin.

Another accident, Dad would say. Shame coiled around me like a snake, squeezing the breath from my chest.

"Get up!" Jeff yanked at my hair, dragging me to my feet. "Someone's coming."

Wiping my face, I forced myself to breathe. I couldn't let her win—not like this. Reaching for the grassy bank, I grasped a clump of weeds, pulling myself up while brushing down my clothes. This isn't the real Jeff, I've done this. This mess is my fault.

I always made excuses for Jeff. It was my nagging, I told myself, that made him snap. He'd come around, apologise, and beg for my forgiveness like always. But right now, there was nothing—no reaction, no emotion. Just cold silence. I had to remember—it's *all* my fault, anyway. Despite everything, he was still the one I loved.

I reached up to touch him, hoping for a sign of forgiveness, some small gesture to make things right. After hesitating he took my hand, and I limped alongside him, smiling through the pain, scolding myself. I asked for this. I didn't deserve better.

Mum's eyes nearly popped out of her head. "My god! Lucy, what happened? Let me look at you."

Jeff jumped in before I could answer, his voice flat and rehearsed. "She's clumsy, aren't you, Babe? Fell down the embankment. Took two of us to pull her back up."

I avoided her gaze. "It's not as bad as it looks. I'll go upstairs and get changed."

Mum wasn't buying it. Her eyes flicked between Jeff and me, suspicion creeping in making her tone razor-sharp. "How come you're not muddy, Jeff, if you helped her?"

Jeff shuffled, blind to her concern, already weaving his next lie. "My friend Becky got muddy. I held onto the lamppost so she could get to Lucy. Isn't that right, Babe?" His eyes locked onto mine, daring me to contradict him.

I swallowed hard, guilt for lying and shame weighing down on me making my words tremble. "Yeah, that's right, Mum."

An hour later, Dad came home from work. I could hear him and Mum whispering in the kitchen, voices hushed and strained. I held my breath until they stopped.

Mum called out, "Dinner's ready when you are."

At the table, Dad tried to make conversation as if everything was fine and completely ignored the bruises on my face and my limp. "How was your day?"

What could I say? Oh, you know, Dad, just the usual—got kicked around a bit, made excuses for Jeff, lied to Mum again. Instead, I forced a smile, pushing the words past the lump in my throat. "Fine. Just fine."

He turned his attention to Jeff. "If you've got time later, could you help me at the depot? I've got some deliveries to make."

"Sure, no problem. We'll leave the girls to chat. I'll head to the station on the way back, if that's okay with you, Babe?"

Something about his false concern and deference sent a spark of anger through me. His voice, soft and careful, played the part of the caring partner so perfectly that it almost fooled me—well almost. But I knew better. Beneath the surface, where my love for him burned, something darker festered. I hated how much I craved his approval, how the thought of losing him filled me with panic, yet I couldn't forget what had happened earlier.

"Yes of course. What time will you be back?" What else could I say? Hey, if you so much as touch her I won't just boil a bunny!

"Not sure. Don't wait up."

Don't wait up! What did that mean? My chest tightened. He planned to stay out late, probably with her... hippy Becky. Or maybe with someone else entirely—who knew how many women he was stringing along?

I nodded, trying to appear nonchalant, but inside, anger crumbled and self-loathing arose. I knew what he was doing, I knew he was slipping away, but what could I do? Confront him? He'd just twist it; make it like I was paranoid or clingy. Maybe I am. Maybe I deserved this.

A lump stuck in my throat, my head throbbed with unspoken fears. Why did I bother asking? I knew he wouldn't come home. And if he did, I'd just be waiting here, pretending everything was fine, pretending I wasn't dying inside.

I forced a smile and swallowed the knot in my throat. I couldn't lose him. Not yet. Not like this.

Dad returned around nine o'clock, grabbed a beer, and went straight upstairs for a bath. I sat alone, restless and worried, unable to shake the dread creeping up my spine.

In the morning, Jeff still hadn't come back. By noon, my anxiety was unbearable. Borrowing Mum's car, I drove to the old station though I could have run there in fifteen minutes.

Switching off the engine I heard familiar sounds: laughter, the jingle of glasses, and Lance's guitar strumming. As I entered the building, I lost myself in the music and the memories of belonging. But then reality crashed in, and I burst into the waiting room. Two guys were shooting up, another eating Coco Pops. Lance was hunched over, head down.

"Has anyone seen Jeff? He didn't come home last night." My voice sounded feeble even to me.

Lance concentrated on rolling his next spliff. The others, high and delirious, laughed about red shoes and Tonto, oblivious to my desperation.

With frustration boiling over I clenched my teeth. "Come on, you're not in the Masons. Has anyone seen him?"

Lance glanced up, adjusting his glasses. "I've not been around much and I've not seen him in days, which is odd for him, he normally searches me out. Guess he's been busy… if you know what I mean, wink wink."

"Where's Becky?" Dreading the answer my fists clenched and unclenched.

He shrugged, polishing his glasses. "She split last night. Said this place was a waste of her time and headed to London. No one's missing the incense, but she was easy on the eyes, if you know what I mean."

The guys erupted in laughter. Nothing able to break their drug-induced haze.

My voice cracked as I fought back tears. "If you see Jeff, tell him to come home."

Lance's tone softened as he took in my lumps and bruises. "Wouldn't waste your breath on him. He's a player, and he's got a temper to match. You deserve better." He paused and threw me a wink. "I'd give you a ride anytime if you want a real man."

I had to get out. I couldn't stay there, not with them laughing, not with all those reminders of how I'd lost him. My sanctuary… but it wasn't mine anymore, was it? Tears blurred my vision as I ran, hitting the tracks beneath my feet as if they could lead me anywhere but here.

Standing by the disused tracks, I stared at the storm brewing in the sky. Even the clouds were angry, I thought, watching them eat away at the hills I used to love. But the darkness? Somehow, it suited me. For the first time in days, my breath slowed, and I let a small, bitter smile tug at my lips. Maybe this was what I deserved.

Driving home later, I clung to the wheel, the silence stretched out and the emptiness expanded within me. Parked on the drive, I found myself staring at the door, hoping—no, needing—him to come back. He had to show up. He always did. He'd be sorry. He'd fix this. But I went inside alone.

As the days passed, my bruises healed. And with each fading mark, my hope for him dimmed too. But even after everything, I knew I'd take him back in a heartbeat. What did that say about me? A hollow laugh escaped my lips. I'm that desperate.

If you would like to read the whole story, then please check out Driven to Kill – a psychological thriller.

https://www.amazon.co.uk/Driven-Kill-Captivating-Psychological-Thriller-ebook/dp/B0DJFZFPGH

https://www.amazon.com/Driven-Kill-Captivating-Psychological-Thriller-ebook/dp/B0DJFZFPGH

Together, Through the Fog

LIVING THROUGH THE FIRST lockdown felt like being on a desert island—at first, a novelty, with family games, endless TV, bike rides, and a dash of that classic British grit. As the days turned into weeks, the novelty wore thin, but our sense of humour held up.

In the worst moments, I was crushed by the thought... life had to be better than this! In the best moments, I cherished that we were making memories we'd treasure forever. Taking part in community spirit whenever we could was an experience I'd never undo.

We laughed and took bets on when my phone, always on full volume and kept close, would erupt with the buzz of my first NHS volunteer duties. "Maybe today?" my husband would say, and it became a running joke as I checked it religiously. No one called, but I knew I was ready.

From the outside, everything looked fine. In reality, our family was weathering the unique storm of having an adult child with mental health challenges in close quarters. Tensions had always ebbed and flowed, but in lockdown, everything seemed amplified. My daughter, battling her own dark thoughts, grew increasingly agitated, critical, and negative, especially towards me. I knew her frustration ran deep, but no matter what I said, it always seemed wrong.

At times, I caught myself snapping and immediately regretted it, knowing that her words came from a place of pain. Still, it was hard not to feel suffocated by her unending cycle of hurt. I'd search my soul, wondering if I was at fault, if there was something I could do better. Yet, my love and apologies never seemed enough to restore the peace we all longed for.

One particularly tense weekend, she accused me of 'driving her away,' her face crumpled in tears. "Why can't I stay longer? All my friends are with their parents—why am I different?" she asked, her voice rising in frustration. I wanted to say yes, but I feared our fragile peace would shatter completely. She threatened to leave, and part of me wondered if it might help, but I always worried she'd spiral, that she'd be alone and vulnerable.

Sadly, these issues were not new—only heightened. The previous year had seen us rushing to help her several times. Love is patient, love is kind... but fear that she might self-harm overruled everything.

"My counsellor told me I don't need any more help, I just need more support," she said.

I'd have liked to meet this counsellor! I became so browbeaten that I even offered to leave home myself. Self-preservation screamed at me to run away. My daughter wasn't the only one who needed help. I wondered if her counsellor was free. No part of me remained strong, or whole.

Where was the sweet person we'd raised? Had she gone forever?

Everyone around her was trying to help. No one had the right skills. Only a willingness and desire to change deep within her would bring her peace. But she was deaf to our loving advice. And so, I gave in to her threats; I told her I loved her and apologised for anything I might have said that offended her over the weekend. She agreed to stay until the next day. The crying stopped, and I saw we were back on the treadmill, unable to step off.

Late that night, as everyone else slept, I found myself pouring my heart into an email to MIND, the mental health charity. I didn't hold back. I described the tears, the blame, and the tension that was fraying the bonds of our family. I clicked send, and a weight lifted off me simply by sharing our story.

The next day, Nick from MIND called. His voice was calm and kind as he listened, allowing me to explain without judgement. When he spoke, he was firm but encouraging. "She's an adult, and she must take responsibility for her actions," he said. "She needs to realise that if she doesn't make changes, your relationship might break down. Tough love may be hard, but she can't ignore that others have needs too. Talk to your daughter together; tell her how you're feeling. Explain the stress you're both under and that to continue supporting her, you need to see improvement."

I hung up with renewed energy, a flicker of hope brightening the fog. That evening, I shared Nick's words with the rest of the family, and we sat together for the first time, really opening up about our feelings. Each of us had been trapped, unable to voice how her struggles were affecting us all. It was a relief to speak honestly, to admit we were hurting too. My husband decided he also needed help and called MIND for advice. After his call, we had an emotional heart-to-heart, recognising that we needed to look after each other and act as one voice when we spoke to our daughter.

The next day, she returned home for a short stay. When the inevitable tears and arguments began again, we were better prepared. We spoke calmly, sharing that her struggles, while valid, were affecting all of us. We told her we loved her, that we'd support her, but that the family couldn't continue this way. It wasn't easy, but she listened. In that moment, we began to rebuild the boundaries that would keep us close while giving everyone room to breathe.

With MIND's support, our family has found a new understanding. Together, we've set a plan in place—a way for us all to coexist, respect each other's space and support each other without losing ourselves. Children are our life force, but we can't allow them to control us or their siblings—no matter their illness.

In those early lockdown days, our world had crumbled as we lived a waking nightmare. Thank goodness for love, laughter, and patience. And God bless all those who work at MIND, delivering their wisdom with such gentle and straightforward advice.

Now, I see that even during the toughest times, hope can grow back stronger than before. We pulled together as a family and brought forth the fruit of love, learning that hugs often speak louder than words.

During COVID-19 and isolation, the full impact of living with someone with mental health issues took its toll on our family. Thanks to community support and the chance to speak with people who'd faced similar challenges, we received advice on the way forward. I believe it isn't too late to repair the damages caused by lockdown, for we've learned that without a firm foundation, nothing will last.

MIND's UK support line: 0300 102 1234

He’s off the wall!

CORPORATE ENTERTAINMENT, football matches, new faces, and a good meal—nothing too out of the ordinary, right? But life has a funny way of turning even the simplest events upside down.

It wasn’t until halftime during the Aston Villa vs. Derby game that I noticed Rob. He was my colleague’s client, deeply engaged in a chat with a woman named Joanne. Our paths crossed on the stairs, and we got to talking football as we wandered off to place a few bets. Rob, however, missed the mark and nearly dragged me into the gents’ by mistake. Not exactly ideal! But as a seasoned account manager, I laughed it off. He was ‘off the wall,’ after all.

In the second half, our conversation took on a new level. Rob was intrigued by my recent gliding experience and asked for the number of the club so he could try it. We discovered we were both wading through messy divorces—he with a football-loving son, Alan, and me with a lively Border Collie named Rigsby, who had a taste for cheese on toast and plenty of attitude.

I emailed him the gliding club’s number, unsure if I’d hear back. When he did reply, the exchange quickly turned into light-hearted back-and-forth banter, and soon, I found myself eagerly checking my inbox.

Our first date was at the romantic Windsor Tiffin in Burbage, where he arrived with chocolates, wine, and flowers. We talked until early morning, laughing about everything—even Rigsby’s antics. But our second date at the Saracen's Head in Shirley a place not known for its ambience or great food was… well, less than charming. Halfway through, Rob casually mentioned another son, Rex.

Confused, I said, "I thought you only had one son named Alan?"

"No," he chuckled, "I've got three boys—Liam, Alan, and Rex. Alan's the football fan." So, he'd left out two kids in our previous chats! Still, the more he spoke about his family, the clearer it became that he was a devoted dad who split custody 50/50, managing it all with a senior role at Aon. I was impressed.

The next date was a family affair with me and Rigsby joining Rob and the boys at their place in Dorridge for a game of table football. Letting the kids win was mandatory—these boys were competitive and didn't like losing! I knew then that I was on to a good thing.

Soon after, Rob invited me on a last-minute trip to Egypt.

My Catholic mum was horrified—"It's too soon!" she said, expressing her concern that he might be after my money. My mortgage was high and my cash flow low, but I knew she meant well.

Despite a few nerves and multiple 'what-ifs,' the holiday was an adventure. A hot-air balloon over the Valley of the Kings, a camel ride along the Nile, and a late-night kalesh journey with a local driver, Ahmed, who introduced us to his family at 2 a.m.—it was wild, spontaneous, and unforgettable. In hindsight, we might reflect on being a tad too trusting.

On our last night, over dinner at an Indian restaurant called Gems, the topic turned to impending divorces and marriage. "Would you get married again?" he asked.

"Yes," I replied.

He leaned in with a mischievous grin, "Would you marry me then?"

No hesitation, "Yes." It had only been five weeks since our first date, but somehow, it felt right. We knew we'd face challenges, but we also knew it would last.

Back in Birmingham a week later, we designed a white gold ring. We kept the engagement a secret for six months to ensure we were making the right decision, dodging a few close calls whenever people dropped by unexpectedly and spotted the ring. We became superstitious about jinxing our happiness, the secrecy added an edge of fun and daring to our relationship, then one day, we knew it was time to share our good news.

A little concern nagged at me. "What if the boys are against us marrying, what if it was too soon?"

"The boys love you and will be delighted, I promise you."

What could go wrong?

In November, we planned a special evening to break the news to the boys over a Chinese meal in Dorridge.

Rob waited until dessert arrived. "We have some big news—Jill and I are engaged, and we're getting married next year!"

The boys' eyes lit up, their excitement peppered with questions: Would we get a bigger house? New rooms? Maybe a pool? 'Realistic' was clearly not in their vocabulary!

As Rob stepped away briefly, six-year-old Rex, the youngest, leaned in and whispered, "You know he's been married before, don't you?"

Feigning surprise, I played along, "Really?"

Apprehensive and concerned, he chewed his lip. "You don't know?"

The boys' ashen faces made me relent. "Of course, I know—and it doesn't matter a bit."

Rob returned, smiling at our grinning faces. "What did I miss?"

"Nothing important," we said in unison, sealing a new beginning with laughter and shared love, knowing our life together would always be a little off the wall.

A Day to Remember. We Gave It a Go!

I FLICK THROUGH my albums, crammed with snapshots of past street parties and celebrations—pictures of the Silver Jubilee, World Cup Willie 1966, the Golden Jubilee 2002, and others. Every one of them looks the same: family and friends gathered all smiles, laughter, song, and a bit of questionable dancing. Tables groan under piles of food, massive tablecloths sag with cake crumbs, and people chatter with everyone, friends and strangers alike. Open invitation—no VIPs here!

Back then, the whole street would gear up. Neighbours spent weeks crafting or buying outfits, gifts, or snacks, and bunting turned every lamppost into a carnival. Mum once made me a red, white, and blue dress topped with a big red bow—made me feel like royalty. For the Golden Jubilee, our family dressed up in velvet hats, draped in patriotic colours, and sat on deckchairs watching the neighbours' rendition of *A Midsummer Night's Dream*. A unique twist, I suppose, but it's the atmosphere that stuck with me—everyone in high spirits, dodgy jokes flying, and enough noise to wake the next town.

These days, weekly NHS claps have become our new chance to meet the neighbours, though always from a safe two-metre distance. One Thursday, I had the bright idea to throw a street party the next day. The neighbours took one look and muttered something about 'the wrong side of town'—guess they weren't as keen.

Friday dawned bright, and we started the day by moving Rob's 'lockdown plants project' from the kitchen to the garden, reclaiming some counter space. Those seedlings, delicate as they were, had been hogging the kitchen table every night for weeks. My once-organised kitchen had begun to look like a scene from a gardening show gone wrong. I felt like my gran, who always managed to turn her cosy little house into a workshop of some sort. Thank goodness Rob had the foresight to plan a hobby—just in case.

Around eleven, we gathered for the two-minute silence marking the 75th anniversary of VE Day. The only noise came from Sandi the gerbil as she scurried around in the shredded paper searching for pieces of carrot and courgette. There was a sense of occasion as we honoured the servicemen and women. The Prince of Wales and the Duchess of Cornwall led the silence, though this year, no crowds—just them, looking thoughtful, and all of us in our own homes.

After that, we got back to the seedlings. Lunchtime meant samosas and toasties, the family staple. Rex, up to his eyes in revision for his BSc, retreated back to his room to study, hoping his hard work would pay off. Meanwhile, Alan and Gemma decided to head to Baddesley Clinton for a walk, and Rob and I took a stroll from Shirley to Dickens Heath, letter in hand. Along the way, we passed neighbours in their front gardens, drinks in hand, bunting waving, and old-fashioned teacups brimming with... something stronger than tea.

"Nice bunting!" we called to one family. They grinned and waved back. We spotted an A0 poster outside a house, all about VE Day—a clear home-schooling project, or maybe a masterpiece by an eager parent. We stopped to read it, grateful that the history still held meaning today.

On our way home, we stopped by Rob's dad's flat. At eighty-nine, he's been isolating, though he came to the window for a chat. Loneliness aside, he's keen for the PM's update on Sunday, hoping it'll bring a bit of freedom. He shared memories of his own VE Day, celebrating with a bonfire on Birmingham's Belgrave Highway, where he and a mate, Micky Pardo, threw anything burnable on the flames. It was a wild day, he said, full of joy and the promise of better times.

Back home, dinner prep started—a pasta bake alongside a roast chicken, with a few veg on the side. By now, I'd donned a red, white, and blue outfit, ready for Gareth Malone's *Zoom Choir* sing-along. The plan was to belt out *White Cliffs of Dover* and *We'll Meet Again,* but just as I warmed up, we discovered that Gemma's gerbil, Sandi, had passed away. Poor Gemma was heartbroken, her first encounter with death. The house grew solemn, plans for a gerbil funeral whispered between us. Singing didn't seem right, so I skipped the choir.

After putting the chicken in for dinner, we head out for our daily exercise around Brueton Park and pass a street party in Blythe Way. The whole street is out and there is even a band playing, no wonder it is a place I would be happy to move to.

People are friendlier these days, acknowledging each other as they pass by maybe even stopping for polite conversation. We are united, joined together by events around us. An elderly lady sits on a bench and opens her sandwiches. People greet her as they pass by. I wonder what her story is. Was she involved in the war or part of the celebrations seventy-five years ago? Two young mums play cricket with their children and a family of four out on bicycles passes by. We head home hand-in-hand, a part of something memorable.

Dinner came and went and conversation turned to the family's next challenge—a five-hundred-mile cycling trek.

Plates cleared, Gemma left for her dad's to lay Sandi to rest, and Liam, our dinner guest, headed home with dreams of transforming his balcony into an oasis.

The night rolled on with two Zoom calls, first with Rob's sisters, then with mine. Lively chatter filled the screens as we swapped VE Day memories and pondered Boris's upcoming announcement. The Queen's speech capped the evening at nine, reminding us that, despite it all, the nation's spirit endures, and our streets, though empty, brim with kindness and resilience.

Her words:

"But our streets are not empty; they are filled with the love and the care that we have for each other. And when I look at our country today and see what we are willing to do to protect and support one another, I say with pride that we are still a nation those brave soldiers, sailors and airmen would recognise and admire."

As the curtain fell on this VE Day, Vera Lynn's *We'll Meet Again* echoed on our screens, sung by NHS frontliners from across the country. Different times, different heroes—but some things, it seems, never change.

NHS Volunteer—Waiting for that First Buzz

It's sunny outside, so why am I wary?
I might make a mistake—that's what's scary.
It's cold indoors; I pull my dressing gown tight,
Being 'on call,' I expect calls tonight.
Adrenaline pumps as I wait with care,
Wondering who's out there, needing repair.

Spring's on its way, so why am I cold?
A lone daffodil sways, making out it's bold.
My first ringtone startles, I check to see—
How's the shift going, who needs me?
On duty, yes, but no ringing elation—
Instead, in the garden, I face weed vexation!

The screen lights up: Imogen's better, she'll be alright.
A small win for NHS in the COVID-19 fight!
Summer's for picnics, sunscreen, and cheer,
But this year feels different, predictions unclear.
A call from a lady, I ask, "Are you alright?"
Needs are simple, a prescription required, she's fading away.

Take a walk in the garden; it may brighten your day,
Get some fresh air, but keep two meters away!
Volunteers will bring her meds by tonight.
She's grateful, reassured, a bit lighter inside,
There's hope in her voice and warmth in the light.
Maybe we'll beat this COVID-19—eradication in sight.

Pigs are Super Smart, Aren't They?

IT STARTED OFF like any ordinary summer's day on shift. The sun was blazing, and most sensible folk were gearing up for BBQs, ready to bask in the heat. And there was me—stuck inside, wishing I'd booked the day off. Instead of sizzling in the sun like other people, a sense of dread brewed inside me that something was bound to go wrong today.

Working on the high-pressure gas pipeline system is thrilling and nerve-racking—a proper emergency service gig! The system itself is a maze of underground pipelines, a bit like roads and motorways for gas, with multi-junctions (MJs) acting as traffic lights, 'bus stops' where the gas hops onto slower lines, and compressor stations to keep it all moving. Today, Adam was managing everything north of the Midlands, while I was in the sunny southern half.

Sunday's maintenance day, so it's usually quieter—most of the gas-hungry sites are off. We were sending a couple of 'intelligent PIGs' down two sections to check for faults. What could possibly go wrong, right?

Now, let me clear this up: they're not actual pigs. Pipeline pigs are chunky, steel contraptions designed to inspect for defects, and if they were on roads, they'd be laying down smart motorways. Fat, lazy, and costly—get it wrong, and you might just see pigs fly!

The ground team phoned Adam, ready to launch his pig up north, and he lowered the pressure in that direction. My pig was launched down south toward the Midlands, everything set. We thought it was going to be easy. But twenty minutes later, Adam's face went ghostly white.

"Adam, what's up?" our supervisor asked, eyes flicking to the monitors.

"The pig hasn't passed the marker—it's ten minutes late," Adam said, voice tight with worry.

"Check pressures, demand North and South," our supervisor said, frowning. "Hold on—Cunningham's taking gas. I thought they were off today?"

Adam's eyes widened. "They are, but they're on the pig's route. It's bypassed the MJ and is now headed south instead of north—straight for the Midlands!"

I shot up. "Which part of the Midlands? I've got a pig due through Solihull in twenty!"

Our supervisor looked like he'd aged a decade. "Demand's pushed the pig faster—it's speeding toward Wolverhampton." He picked up the Red Phone, issuing evacuation orders for the shopping centre near valve 89, in case the gas escaped and lit up like a bonfire.

Adam was sweating as he shut down bus stops and MJs to clear a path, knowing what was at stake. I was frantically working with my ground crew to manually divert my pig, but Adam's was barrelling towards a head-on collision with mine.

The implications started to hit us. Up the Solihull pipeline, there's a chemical plant, the new HS2 Interchange, and the M42 packed with traffic. Worse, if things really went south, Birmingham Airport and the NEC could also be in the line of fire. It was a catastrophe waiting to happen.

Our supervisor made the call: "We're going to have to crash them. Better in a field than risking the airport. Prepare for impact at Favenshaw; it's rural enough."

Tension was thick in the control room as we all scrambled to slow Adam's pig. My pig hurtled towards Solihull while police and the army cleared routes and evacuated roads. All hands were on deck.

Then came the newsflash: "As the pigs collided, a thunderous bang echoed through Favenshaw. The Smith family, out for a BBQ, saw a fireball rise over a field. They're fine but taken in for a check-up."

The helicopter pilot called in. "Looks like two roasted pigs. What's the cost of those?"

Our supervisor shook his head, relieved. "Half a million. But no fatalities."

As the ground team cleared out the charred pigs, one of them radioed back, "Well, they're fried alright."

Back in the control room, we all let out a sigh of relief. Questions would come, and maybe a few P45s, but we'd done everything we could.

"Anyone for a bacon sandwich?" I asked, smirking.

"When pigs fly!" they all laughed.

Three in a Basket

Three adventurers set off in a basket so high,
Floating through clouds, up into the sky.
They're off to explore, wherever they please,
From jungles and deserts to tropical seas!

With a compass, a map, and spirits so free,
Yet all they can think of is a nice cup of tea.
"India's lovely," says one with a grin,
"But where's a kettle? Let's find an inn!"

"France is delightful, with pastries and more,
But a cuppa, I'd say, is what we're here for."
Even in Africa, warm and so bright,
They're peeking for teapots from morning till night.

Through hills and valleys, from mountains to shores,
They sail on, still dreaming of English tea stores.
At last, they decide with a bit of a fuss—
Exploring is grand, but tea is a must!

A little bit memoir, A little made up
A lot of fun!

Did he have a Plan B?

CHARLES WAS YOUR typical bloke. He had a wife who adored him, four fantastic kids, a brown Border Collie named Jack, and the inevitable mortgage. He was a local councillor, a member of the running club, and a proper 'Mr Nice Guy'—the sort of fellow you'd trust to mind your keys. Only, Charles had a secret side.

By day, he wore the badge, serving as a policeman in Birmingham. But often, he was away for weeks on undercover gigs, roaming the seedier parts of town. He'd vanish at odd hours to take calls or meet 'colleagues.' When friends questioned his absences, Charles's wife would shrug and wave it off, assured it was all part of his work.

Yet somehow, Charles managed to be everything to everyone. His kids saw him as a hero, he was the king of backyard BBQs, and his spice garden was the envy of the neighbourhood. How he found the time was a mystery, but no one questioned it. We might've noticed something off—the wandering eyes, the too-good-to-be-true charm—but no one said a word.

Then he retired. For the first time, Charles was fully 'there,' and it seemed like the family was finally getting the best of him. He took up consulting gigs in security and training, still disappearing on occasion, but not as often. Life settled into a comfortable rhythm.

Until the night we ran into him at the Slug and Lettuce, having drinks with a woman we didn't recognize. "Just a work thing," he said, gesturing to an invisible crowd. Odd, but we let it go.

Over the next two years, he set up a home office, basking in his new domestic life. But then, trouble started creeping in. His eyesight was failing, and he was getting forgetful. We chalked it up to stress, maybe ageing, until his diagnosis came through: early-onset dementia. The news hit hard, as he was only fifty-years-old, but Charles, ever the stoic, brushed it off. "I'll live for today," he said.

His behaviour changed. The man who once lit up every room grew withdrawn, more lost by the day. And then the real bombshell dropped. Out of the blue, Charles announced he was leaving—packing his bags for an old flame he'd reconnected with on Friends Reunited. His wife and kids were blindsided, and when he finally moved in with his long-lost school sweetheart, we all tried to make sense of it.

Sadly, our get-togethers no longer included Charles. We heard that his health was declining, but he was happy with his new life. He went on holidays with his girlfriend and saw his children less and less as his eyesight deteriorated, which made navigating the trains and buses needed to visit them hard.

Months passed, and life went on. Charles drifted further from his old family, his health slipping faster than anyone expected. Then came the day his wife, tidying up the loft, was befuddled by an old folder tumbling from the roof beams. Inside? A diary. Not just any diary, but Charles's confession—a record of countless affairs spanning decades, including a long-term relationship with someone just a few streets over.

Turns out, he'd been parking his car a mile from home, telling his wife he couldn't bring it close due to undercover work. His mistress never saw anything suspicious, so they carried on without a hitch. Now, with his mind faltering, he'd forgotten all about the diary, leaving it as a final gift for his wife.

Sadly, finding details of all his indiscretions meant they overshadowed any happy times they'd had together.

Devastated, she took stock. The man she'd once loved had woven an entire second life behind her back. Suddenly, his request for a divorce made sense, and she saw the years with new eyes. But fate twisted the knife yet again: just as he was preparing to marry his old flame, she fell seriously ill, leaving Charles in a care home while she sought treatment. She never recovered from the cancer, and Charles found himself alone, trapped in the very life he'd chosen.

Now, he sits in the care home—a relatively young man in a sea of much older residents, lamenting his isolation. He wants to go home, to be looked after, and to feel less alone. But the bridge to his old life had burned, and his wife—who might once have cared for him without hesitation—now sees him for who he truly is.

And his wife? Well, she can finally move forward, wiser and free from the shadow of his secret life. Duty would have kept her caring for him twenty-four/seven with no life of her own. Reading the diaries gave her an escape valve and she took it. His kids still visit him, with the knowledge that he's safe, even if he's unhappy.

Did Charles somehow know this would happen? Did he tuck away that diary as a Plan B, a way for his family to finally know the truth and, perhaps, find freedom? We'll never know.

My Dad, the Secret Star

MY DAD WAS a Black and White Minstrel back in the day, and when he first arrived in England, he wrote jokes for well-known comedians and songs for a popular female solo singer. He'd sworn to keep their identities secret… that is until he told me! Was that a mistake?

Dad was modest, not one to boast. We even made a pinkie promise when I was young, vowing I'd never reveal the names of the stars he worked for. Locking our little fingers, I knew—even then—that the promise was serious and sacred. This was a secret I'd take to my grave. Or could I?

Relatives, hoping for a bit of insider information, would offer all sorts of bribes—a new bike, extra money from the tooth fairy, even a new sister. One day after school, I spotted a reporter lurking by the gates. He'd heard the rumours of Dad's fame and must've thought a bag of sweets could buy me. "Not me, mister," I said, running to get the principal. A pinkie promise is a pinkie promise!

The reporter argued, "The story deserves to be told," but I held my ground. More reporters came, tempting me with bigger rewards, but I never gave in. I knew that in the olden days, breaking a pinkie promise could cost you a finger. Dad wouldn't have taken my finger, but the sadness in his eyes would've been harder to bear.

Life settled down; the reporters stopped calling, and Dad went on living two lives—the secret writer and the humble engineer. Stars stopped visiting our home, worried the press would find out that Dad was the real wit behind many number-one hits and top comedians' jokes.

Sometimes, I'd forget my promise and start sharing stories with friends—like the tricks Dad performed with his harmonica and squeezebox—before catching myself. The promise still held, even after Dad passed away.

One memory that makes me smile is when Dad mimicked Harry Worth's famous shop window trick at home. With one arm and leg raised, he'd stand by the wardrobe, creating the illusion he was levitating. It was hysterical. You might be wondering if I've just broken my promise but I can assure you Harry Worth wasn't one of them. He was a funny guy and we loved watching him.

The Fez

One day, a parcel arrived from my sister in Hinckley. It wasn't my birthday and I wondered what was inside. I was flying to Canada and knew the postage would be cheaper before I left. Had she found something while clearing out Mum's house?

Ripping off the bubble wrap, I found a note from Dad. He'd died years ago and my heart melted when I spotted his handwriting: *We never made a pinkie promise about this, so here it is... just like that!* My heart skipped a beat—it can't be what I thought it was, can it?

Instantly, I was transported back to my parents' old house in Burbage, watching Dad play the Squeezebox when I spotted a bag atop the wardrobe.

"What's in the bag?" I'd asked.

"Little Miss Nosey!" he teased, pulling out a red hat with a black tassel on top. "It's a fez," he said, placing it on his head with a flourish. "Just like that!" He threw his arms out wide, laughing. His joy was contagious, and soon I was laughing too, demanding my own turn. "Just like that!" I'd mimicked, basking in the thrill. Dad then gave me a little acting lesson.

"A comedian named Tommy Cooper had a famous catchphrase," Dad explained. "Know what it is?"

"Just like that!" I yelled.

"Exactly! Tommy Cooper's fez and his saying made him famous worldwide. Even in Turkey today, market traders sell fezzes, calling out, 'Just like that!' But here's a secret most people don't know: fezzes were once banned in Turkey. Your great-great-grandfather smuggled this one out of the country. Look inside—the label says 'Made in the Imperial Istanbul Fez Factory, 1920.'"

I remember running my fingers gently over the red felt, its history almost tangible beneath my touch.

"In 1925, Mustafa Kemal Atatürk, Turkey's new president, wanted Turkey to be more European. He thought fezzes held the country back, so he banned them and made people wear Western hats instead. That's when your great-grandfather smuggled his fez out of Turkey. It passed down to me when your granddad died."

"I love it, Dad. Can I have it one day?"

"Maybe," Dad said with a smile. "But I won't make a pinkie promise."

When my sister found the fez and Dad's note while clearing out Mum's house, it felt like a piece of him was with us again. I put the fez on my head, threw my arms wide, and called out, "Just like that!"

And with the fez, I knew I'd always keep our pinkie promise.

Rutland Water – the Tipping Point

WE'D KNOWN MARK and Alice for years, and they'd often regaled us with tales of sailing through exotic waters, navigating vibrant coastlines under open skies. Both seasoned sailors, they'd invited us to join them for a day on Rutland Water, a popular reservoir nestled in England's countryside. With their experience, we figured, what could possibly go wrong?

Rutland Water, one of Europe's largest artificial lakes, has a certain charm. The sprawling reservoir, fed by the rivers Nene and Welland, supplies water to the East Midlands and is surrounded by a twenty-six-mile cycling route. On sunnier days, Rob and I would join the Desford Peddlers Cycling Club, dressing in vintage outfits, pedalling around the lake, and stopping at pubs along the way. But today was different; today, we'd be on the water.

When we arrived, Mark and Alice were readying the boat in their waterproofs, a sleek but surprisingly small sailing dinghy. Alice waved, explaining she'd stay ashore to prepare our picnic. The sky was overcast, and rain pattered steadily, casting a grey pall over the lake, but Mark seemed unfazed.

"The rain should clear up soon," Mark assured us. "The water's choppy, but the conditions are still good. Rob, I'll take you out first for a quick spin, and then it'll be your turn, Jill."

Rob and I exchanged an excited glance. Still, I couldn't help eyeing the lake's restless waves, my nerves tightening as Mark handed us wetsuits, sailing boots, and buoyancy aids. He pointed to the clubhouse for us to change, urging us to hurry before the weather worsened. Ten minutes later, Rob was climbing aboard with Mark, who shouted back to us, "We'll be about twenty minutes!"

Rob nodded at the boat. "Sleek sailing dinghy, but it looks quite fragile, will it be safe on this choppy water?"

"Yes, of course, I've been out many times, nothing to worry about. Best to go out early as the forecast is not so good later today and we'll want to have our picnic when we come back," said Mark

I'm feeling scared and nervous as I watch them. What if something goes wrong? I've known Mark for years, but the weather seems to be getting worse.

Alice and I watched the boat sail toward the centre of the lake. Mark was pointing things out to Rob, gesturing towards the sails and explaining the basics—something about wind and progress and I think I caught… the sailors call that the No Go Zone. Even from a distance, I could tell Rob was thrilled, waving at us with a thumbs-up. But the darkening sky and the steadily increasing wind made me uneasy. I glanced at Alice, who watched the boat with a small frown.

By the time they returned, the water was choppier than before. Rob jumped off the boat, grinning. "That was incredible! Your turn now, Jill."

Feeling a mix of excitement and trepidation, I made my way to the dinghy. Mark checked my gear and, with an easy smile, reassured me. "Let's make it a quick ten minutes."

As we set sail, I felt a spark of exhilaration. I moved across the dinghy as Mark steered, focusing on the wind and the boat's rhythm. Moving from one side of the sailing dinghy to the other was fun. I started to unwind. Why have I got this illogical fear? I can swim, Mark's a sailing professional and I'm wearing safety gear.

Just as I was starting to relax, a sudden gust of wind sent a spray of water across our faces. The sky had darkened further, and Mark's expression shifted.

"We're heading back," he called.

Before we could make much progress, a powerful wave hit the side of the dinghy. With a sudden lurch, we were capsized, thrown into the cold, churning water. I felt the weight of the wetsuit and boots pulling at me, and my buoyancy aid seemed only partially effective. Very quickly I felt helpless.

"Swim toward the dinghy and hold on," Mark shouted.

I kicked and struggled, but the dinghy seemed to drift further with each passing wave. Is today the day that I die? Memories and images from my life flitted through my mind as I fought the urge to give in, until, miraculously, I reached the dinghy. Mark was gripping the side, steadying himself.

Just then, a bright red rescue boat cut through the darkness, its flashing lights a welcome sight. I will survive!

"Do you folks need help? We saw the swell hit your dinghy," a voice shouted down to us.

Mark was already shaking his head, but I found myself yelling, "Yes, please!"

Without hesitation, they pulled me aboard, and I felt a rush of relief as my feet landed on the solid deck. Weak and shivering, I glanced back. Mark looked understandably unhappy, but I didn't care. I stared death in the face and wanted nothing more than to be rescued. Mark righted the dinghy before steering it back to shore.

Back on land, I headed straight for the clubhouse, where Rob was waiting. Seeing me, drenched and visibly shaken, he ran over, his face twisting in concern.

"What on earth happened?" he asked.

I recounted the ordeal, the dark water, the capsized dinghy, the moment I truly thought I might drown. Rob looked horrified, especially at the thought of nearly missing it all while drying off inside.

The next morning, an article in the Rutland News detailed the rescue: *"A woman was saved after a sailing dinghy capsized in the turbulent waters of Rutland Water. She later expressed her gratitude to the rescue team, stating, 'I didn't understand the risks but kept swimming.'"*

Rutland water is normally a big pond, where sailing, windsurfing, kayaking, canoeing or stand-up paddle boarding, offer a perfectly safe environment for beginners through to expert swimmers. But, as with any water sport, the water can be colder than expected, winds severe even in warm weather and hidden currents can trouble the most confident of swimmers.

From that day forward, I've held close a quote by Edwin Louis Cole: *"You don't drown by falling in the water; you drown by staying there."*

Boring Day at the Office, Dear?

MANAGING A GAS Emergency Call Centre involves quick thinking, CPR, and dealing with the unexpected. Were my days boring? You be the judge!

The Call

There are three emergency call centres strategically placed across the UK, and we'd only been operational for four weeks when we received the fateful call.

"There's a bomb in your building; it'll go off in an hour. Evacuate!" said the bomber.

A call agent frantically waved towards me, and I grabbed my headset to listen in.

"What did you say?" asked the agent.

"There's a bomb in your building; evacuate!" the caller repeated.

"Where's the bomb?" I asked.

"Your building. You're wasting my time!" The call disconnected.

"Was it an overflow call?" I asked the stunned call agent.

"I didn't notice," she replied, visibly shaken.

A team leader dashed to the system room to retrieve details of the call and where it might have overflowed from. Was it meant for us?

Our dilemma was clear. Overflow systems ran between Eastwood, Hardcastle, and Nuneaton, meaning the bomb could be in any of our three call centres. Which one should be evacuated?

Evacuating all centres would be unprecedented, and the risks felt enormous. Nonetheless, I dialled our director and connected the police on a three-way call. After a tense discussion, our director gave the order. "Evacuate all call centres. We don't know which site has the bomb due to go off in fifty-five minutes. Get everyone out and have each manager wait by the main entrance for the police, sniffer dogs, and emergency services. Staff should gather at the designated assembly points and leave vehicles behind—they might have bombs attached."

I pressed the emergency evacuation button. Staff activated emergency mode to reroute calls to smaller operational sites, then began filing out. I called the other call centre managers to ensure they evacuated too.

It was a bitterly cold winter's day, and as we gathered outside, the call centre managers set up a Zoom meeting while we waited for police and emergency services.

"Were any of you overflowed to Nuneaton about fifteen minutes ago?" I asked.

"We were," said Eastwood's manager. "It was arranged late yesterday for call handler training."

"We were managing our own calls and handling a few from Eastwood and Nuneaton," said Hardcastle's manager, notably sporting a Hardcastle football strip. I'd have to ask him about that on another day!

The police and sniffer dogs arrived, and unfamiliar with our layout, asked me to guide them through the building, while others searched under cars.

A team leader hurried over, holding up her tablet with call logs. "The caller ID was withheld, but it overflowed from Eastwood, and the caller had a strong Portuguese accent."

"How do you know that?" asked the police.

"He said bombear instead of bomb—Portuguese. I'm learning the language," she replied. What a handy coincidence for all concerned.

The police quickly informed their counterparts at Eastwood, urging them to ensure a full evacuation, with only forty minutes left.

Staff returned to Nuneaton and Hardcastle call centres, taking back control from the smaller operational sites. Though busy, there was a heavy silence and an atmosphere of dread as the clock ticked towards the supposed detonation time.

At Eastwood, the police and sniffer dogs found nothing—just a hoax, it seemed. Staff were cleared to return.

But an hour later, a surge of overflow calls from Eastwood prompted me to ring their manager. No one answered. I turned on the news, a knot tightening in my stomach.

"A bomb has just exploded in the Eastwood emergency call centre, injuring multiple staff; fatalities are unknown. A man was seen fleeing the scene in a navy hoodie, jeans, and white trainers. It is believed that he is Portuguese and had recently been employed as an agency worker. Police are treating this as a terror attack."

I turned off the news and looked around, watching our staff, unaware of the fate of their friends and colleagues at Eastwood. I wondered how any of us could ever smile again.

The Next Emergency

On an ordinary day, engineers were dispatched across the area, handling maintenance and gas leaks. Lee, covering Nottingham, sent Tim to Jubilee Crescent. Tim confirmed his arrival, but when he didn't check in after thirty minutes, Lee grew concerned. As an experienced engineer, Tim knew the drill. Not calling meant that something was wrong.

Lee rang Tim, "Hi Tim, you still there?"

Speaking softly, Tim replied, "I'm in the loft looking for the leak, but there are hundreds of cannabis plants here. The owners were already here and didn't look pleased—they hadn't called us. They're in the garden talking now."

"Get out of there; I'll call the police," said Lee.

"Oh god, they're calling me down—what do I do?" Tim whispered.

"Pretend you haven't seen anything," Lee advised.

"Easier said than done!" Tim murmured as he descended the ladder, leaving his phone line open so we could hear.

"Tim, the police are on their way," I whispered, hoping to reassure him.

We heard a woman scream, "Wāng pụ̄n lng, Akio, k̄heā kląw!" (Put the gun down, Akio—he's scared.)

Tim’s voice wavered, “I didn’t see anything, no gas leak. I’ll just go. Control will contact me if I don’t check in.”

Akio, “Chair. Move faster.”

We could hear Tim moving.

The line cut off after Akio’s voice barked out orders, “Achara, rạb thorṣ̄ạphth̒ k̄hxng k̄heā læ̂w thub mạn!” (Achara, get his phone and smash it.)

The police, on standby, evacuated neighbouring houses and surrounded the area, keeping a low profile while they planned Tim’s rescue. After repeating the call to the police, I started praying. We had Tim’s emergency contact details and a picture of his wife and kids. I had to make them aware of the situation, that part of the job sucked!

Using infrared cameras, they located three people in the kitchen. The helicopter overhead reported substantial heat coming off the loft and upper floor and then moved off quickly to avoid suspicion. Soon, the police entered the house and, through a cracked wall, spotted Tim tied up with Akio waving a gun at him. Akio didn’t see the police enter but, as he noticed them outside, turned his gun back on Tim.

The officers silently advanced. A shot rang out as they reached the kitchen. Had Tim been shot?

Thankfully, it was Achara who fell, while Akio was swiftly subdued, although not without attempting to turn the gun on himself.

Tim was free and, though shaken, called his wife, visibly tearful. He thought he wouldn’t be leaving there alive.

As the police filled us in later, they'd uncovered a commercial-sized cannabis farm worth over a million pounds, the largest in Warwickshire. Tim was safe, but he'd just discovered the first of many cannabis farms in the area.

One neighbour said, "It's a quiet residential area and people keep themselves to themselves, the house's rented and we rarely see anyone living there. They don't look after the garden; it's an eyesore!"

Another neighbour said, "I rang the gas emergency number when I smelt gas as I passed the house, I hope I did the right thing. I heard there was a gasman inside."

It had been a close call for Tim and as the police handed him a phone to speak to his wife, tears ran down his face. "I thought I was leaving in a body bag!"

Tim found the first cannabis farm on our patch—it wasn't our last!

Review: So, are my days boring? I'll let you be the judge.

Oh, To Be Sharp

I'VE BEEN HERE for over ten years now. Sitting on the back shelf, covered in dust, I wait, hoping for another chance.

Every week, he arrives promptly at 10 o'clock. He puts on his radio and sings *Danny Boy,* just as the kettle starts whistling. For me, this is a time of anticipation because that's when Mr Nugget puts on his glasses and chooses who he wants today.

We're all standing or lying to attention, waiting. I shake myself, trying to clear the dust so he can see my tangerine glow, my telescopic reach, my (oh dear) love handles. I know… I'm old, but we've been together forever—that must count for something, surely? I used to be his first choice. When did it all go wrong?

I feel like crying. Rusty now, will I ever be chosen again?

A knock at the door.

"Granddad, are you in there?"

"Who is it?" said Granddad—Mr Nugget, as I know him.

"It's me, Ben! I said I'd come by to help you."

"So you did, Ben. Good to see you've come. Must be over fifteen years since your last visit to my sanctuary."

"I've come back from Australia to see you. Are you going to open the door? It's freezing out here."

I hear the creaking door open, and my old blades nearly squeak with excitement when I see Ben. He's older, but he still has those kind eyes—and hopefully, a love of all things old, including me.

"Let's have a cuppa, then we'll tackle the north patch."

"Still the hard taskmaster, eh, Gramps? The north patch has always been the worst."

Mr Nugget chuckles. "I know you like it out there in the wilderness."

"I'll need my faithful friend, then."

"Oh, don't know where they are, to be honest," he says, scratching his head. "Over there—use the long green-handled ones. They're new and work a treat."

"No, I'll search the shelves for the old ones. They were reliable and safe, as you always said."

Running his fingers through his beard, Mr Nugget says, "Yes, they were, until they needed servicing."

"I'll do it, Gramps, if I can find them."

"They're on the top shelf somewhere."

Ben clanks and bangs around, clearly looking for me. They're talking about me! I was made for the north patch; it's what I lived for. But what if I'm too old? I've grown comfortable here, retired, sheltered. Maybe I should be grateful and stop thinking about the olden days…

"Gramps, you could do with a duster," says Ben, coughing.

"You're not in the house now, young man. Just don't tell your grandma," says Mr Nuggets, with a wry smile.

I try to cover myself in dust—heavy, with bulging love handles, am I really ready for this? My dad, Wilkinson, always said, "Be careful what you wish for!"

"I've found them, Gramps. A bit dusty, but all in one piece."

"Well done, Ben. They'll need oiling and fine-tuning if you know what I mean."

"Course, like the old days. These were made for the north patch."

I feel sick. I can't do it, can I? The other tools will laugh at my sorry state. I'm doomed to failure.

But as my first edge slides across the whetstone, I inhale deeply—it's like a half 'short back and sides.' I can't wait for the other edge to be done! And the oil… it takes me to places I haven't been in years.

We head outside, and I spot Mr Potts in the neighbouring allotment. He puts on his glasses and scratches his head.

"Well, I never! What a sight for sore eyes! Not only young Ben, but your trusty shears. North patch today, is it?"

"Yes, Potts—it's the dream team," says Mr Nugget, with a twinkle in his eyes, puffing on his pipe. The jungle drums will be beating today!

"Hello, Mr Potts."

"Morning, Ben. He's missed your help."

Gramps shakes his head, but his expanding chest tells a different story.

As Ben lifts me to the hedge, I feel like I'm on cloud nine. The branches are mine for the taking.

It's been too long, but I still have it. I'm still sharp!

My Computer Friends

RECONNECTING ON FACEBOOK with old friends and colleagues gave me a strange and insightful view into everyone's world. I felt close to them and was forever picking up my phone, looking for snippets of information about where they'd been or where they were going—it was exhausting just trying to keep up!

The sad thing was, their lives seemed so much more exciting than mine. I had to do something about that.

How many 'likes' you had was important. Should I create a story to bolster my rating and make sure my friends cared?

It was my birthday today. How many of my online friends would send a message with flowers, cake, or wine? I had to show how popular I was.

Going out for a meal in the real world now involved taking a picture of my food and posting it on 'What's on my mind.'

Who would be the first to answer? Would I get a 'like' or a red heart? The waiting was deafening and showed how much I treated this world as my family now.

Mary, my best friend's posts had disappeared, and as my confidant, I missed her loud, funny messages. She had a big personality and was trying to get back on the dating scene after a long and bitter divorce. I'd been helping her find a man on Tinder. It was fun, but there were a few surprises.

I said to Jack, my husband, "I don't see any news from Mary—haven't for at least a week. Do you think something has happened to her? Shall I send her a message?"

"No, she's probably out in the real world, enjoying life."

"Don't be so uncaring."

"Didn't you say she had a new man from Leamington?"

"Yes, I know she fancies him."

"Does she?"

Giving him a look with a raised eyebrow, "Yes, she does. But she's never not messaged me before to show me her latest outfit and makeup. It's normally five times a day. I do miss her."

"Perhaps there's something wrong with the Facebook algorithm. I've heard it can drop people off your list of favourites."

"That must be it. I'll send a message to Facebook to see if they can do anything." I smiled broadly. I knew he'd know what to do.

"Try messaging her tomorrow if that doesn't work."

"Thanks, darling, I will."

Anyway, back to Facebook Marketplace. There were items for sale from people I knew.

I glance up from my phone. "Can you remember Terry and June's piano?"

"How could I forget!"

"That Christmas when we went round. Terry played for a couple of hours."

"All out of key! We laughed and got drunk, and then along came baby Emily—not so funny then," Jack said, tickling my waist.

"Get off, why don't you? Anyway, we both dote on Emily now, don't we?"

"Course we do, love. How could you think any different?"

"The piano's up for sixty pounds, not bad, as it was in good condition. Just needs a good tuning," I said, tongue in cheek.

"Perhaps we could ask Terry to teach Emily when she's older!"

The book I threw barely missed his head.

"Watch it, that's a first edition."

Ping

Stopping dead in my tracks, "Well, I never. It's a post from Mary. Talk of the devil! I bet she's been on a short holiday somewhere glamorous. I can't wait to hear all the juicy details."

As I opened the post, I noted a black square with a white border around it. "Come over, Jack, this looks important."

We both looked at the screen: To all Mary's friends on Facebook. I am sorry to inform you that Mary has died, sadly under suspicious circumstances. We are holding a funeral next Wednesday at St Peters, Leamington. Everyone is welcome at the church. Anyone with any information about who Mary was seeing should contact the police urgently on 0123 234 567.

“I can’t go to the funeral, Jack,” I said, with tears running down my face.

“Why not, love?”

“We’ve never actually met,” I whispered, wiping away a tear. A strange pang of fear crept in as I clicked ‘Unfriend’ on Mary’s profile, erasing her history from my page. Just as the screen blinked off, an image of Mary’s last date—my Jack—flashed on the screen, staring straight at me with an unsettling familiarity.

As I looked down at our baby Emily, I felt Jack’s gaze still on me. Chills slithered down my spine. When I glanced up, Jack caught my eye in the reflection of my screen and gave a slow, knowing wink.

Shakespeare in Solihull

HER CRIES COULD be heard far and wide, and as nurses and doctors tried to soothe her, the baby stunned everyone by shouting, "*The lady doth protest too much, methinks.*"

"Well, you would say that wouldn't you?" Mary rolled her eyes. "Remember, *Frailty, thy name is woman.* Where's that good-for-nothing father of yours when I need him?"

Like meerkats, everyone looked towards the ceiling. John Shakespeare's antics were well-documented in Urbs in Rune—a town in the countryside.

Rambling on, Mary said, "At The Beech House, getting drunk if I know him. Talk about *I am one who loved not wisely, but too well*—hence, another mouth to feed! Did you know my good-for-nothing husband has been made redundant from Jaguar Land Rover? I wondered why he got a Range Rover Evoque instead of a cash bonus this year."

"Come on, Mrs Shakespeare, stop mithering. This is a special day. Hold your bonny lad, he's very handsome," said the midwife, passing him to Mary.

Smiling down at her new son, she said, "*Some are born great, some achieve greatness, and some have greatness thrust upon them.* Which will it be for you, my son?"

"Mother, *we know what we are, but know not what we may be.* Give me a break, and a first name, that I may write on this laptop."

"He's very advanced, talking and using a computer already," the doctor remarked in admiration.

"He's wise, there's no doubt about it. I'll call you William, after William the Conqueror."

William spat his dummy out of his mouth, saying, "*Uneasy lies the head that wears the crown.*"

Mary burst into belly laughs, clutching her stomach and wincing in pain. "Don't worry, Wills, your dad will pawn the crown at Cash Generator tomorrow."

Heavy breathing could be heard outside the ward as John hot-footed it in, eager to meet William and Mary. His long curly hair flowed around his waist, and he wore his running gear, sweatband, and orange Reebok trainers. Mary had forgotten he was training for Sunday's Park Run.

"Sorry I'm late, love. *The course of true love never did run smooth.*"

Looking at his son, John said, "You're indeed bonny. My best advice to you is, *we know what we are, but know not what we may be.*"

Mary, getting into her stride, said, "Let's face it, Wills, you'll need to be great, there are lots of bills to pay. Especially if you want to go to Solihull School and become a renowned scholar."

As William lay his head on the pillow, he whispered, "Mum, Dad, *we are such stuff as dreams are made on, and our little life is rounded with a sleep.* Now let me get some sleep."

"Isn't he special, Mary? Can't believe he can talk and is so wise at such a young age. *To be, or not to be, that is the question.* I am so proud of William."

Mary crossed her fingers, smiling with laughter in her eyes. Hallelujah, a child who was going places, a Silhillian and maybe even off to university one day. That would be a first for the family, and it made her proud. As William gripped her finger, she felt a warm glow of pride and grinned at John.

John grinned back—was his luck in?

"Keep your hands to yourself. You'll be seeing the doctor about 'the snip' before I let you near me again."

Will tossed and turned, and in his sleep murmured, *"What's done cannot be undone,"* before smiling and turning over again.

The laughter in the room was infectious, and with hands over their mouths, they gathered together to celebrate the birth.

William loved Solihull School and excelled at English and playwriting. *"We are time's subjects, and time bids be gone."*

But he was a loner and would often be found sitting on his own in the corner of the playground. When asked why he didn't want to play with his peers, he would kick the ground, saying, "I'm hopeless at sport, and they don't like me because I talk too much. *But words are easy, like the wind. Faithful friends are hard to find.*"

The first week of sixth form saw a change in Wills. Mary was astounded when he started showering and using a razor. There was an air of change about him, and she said, "Wills, why shower? It's only Monday morning!"

"Mother, *boldness be my friend.* Girls are now allowed in the sixth form, and I've seen a girl I like. *Nothing will come of nothing,* so I'm trying a new approach at school."

"Well, you are your father's son after all. You'll have no problems in that department. *Look like an innocent flower, but be the serpent under it."*

"That's not me, Mother."

"Remember, *all that glitters is not gold.* I can't wait for you to come home and tell me how you got on."

William thought that girls were silly in comparison to him and preferred the company of sportsmen. Unfortunately, he was but a nerd with his head in a book. By the end of the day, he'd given up. *"Let me be that I am and seek not to alter me."*

Mary was disappointed but for once in her life, kept her counsel.

Eventually, though, at eighteen years old, he found the one—an exam invigilator called Anne Hathaway, eight years his senior. She was small in stature, with a pale complexion, long curly blonde hair, softly spoken, wearing the shortest skirts he'd ever seen, and pink Doc Martens. It was love at first sight!

Feisty and self-assured, he wowed her with his sonnets, charm, and serpent...

His mantra in life became: *All the world's a stage, and all the men and women merely players. They have their exits and their entrances, and one man in his time plays many parts...*

A Great Adventure

Welcome to Paradise
Monteverde, Tortuguero—so much to see,
A holiday of a lifetime,
A tick off the bucket list,
Before the bucket can hit me!

Smiling faces, frowns, confusion—
I'm scared, you see!
Searching, turning pages, faltering words from me.
Hesitant, beaming faces—acceptance, at last.
Hola, la cuenta, por favor,
I can do it, you see!

Confidence grows, new friendships bloom,
A better me!
Memories for a lifetime—
Bartering for souvenirs, vibrant gifts
To grace family homes,
Or be re-gifted to me!

Today, a zipline in the cloud forest—
Scary for me!
Sweating, fear rising like Topsy.
The guide's hand reaches out, a smile lights the way.
Exhilaration, fists in the air!
I made it—no photos, not important, you see.
Memories to last forever will do, for me!

Sounds of the jungle—
Howler monkeys, sloths, birds and more I see.
They call for mates, for prey, and search like me!
I spy a male red-eyed frog who sings competing for love.
She's chosen; his song fades to an end.
It's game over, my friend.
She'll smile,
Another red eye will sing once again.

Biodiversity—the buzzword for eco-travellers like me.
Sustainability, saving the planet—
We're all here, you see… for
A future for children with a world to explore and to be.
We smile, we hold hands—a green bond, we agree.
Let's learn from each other
Before the bucket hits me!

A Bit of a Do

Title: *Hilda's Farewell – **A One-Act Play***

Setting: The basement of a library. It's cold and drab, with no natural light. Large bays of books, a rolling stack, printers, library trolleys, work stationery, and ink stamps fill the room. In one corner, there's a loading bay for transporting books to and from community libraries.

Characters:

- **Jill** – Library Coordinator, aged 54
- **Julia** – Library Trainee, aged 22
- **Joan** – Library Manager, aged 46
- **Hilda** – Team Member, aged 65

(Jill, Julia, and Joan sit around a large table, discussing plans for Hilda's leaving party. Hilda has worked at the library for forty years. She is not present yet.)

JILL

Thanks for helping arrange Hilda's leaving party next month. She's not in until twelve today. Tibbles, her cat, has a vet appointment. So, we've got one hour to brainstorm ideas.

JULIA

I was thinking of an escape room experience in Birmingham. I did the Hellivator escape last week. It's an hour of puzzle-solving, like racing against time. Hilda loves keys and security—I thought it would be perfect!

JOAN

Hellivator? You mean an elevator?

JULIA

Yes, it shakes, rumbles, the floor even moves sideways! You end up holding the walls at times. Quite scary but thrilling!

JILL

But Hilda's heart… it's a bit dodgy. And she's scared of heights.

JULIA

Oh, I'd look after her.

JILL

It's thoughtful, Julia, but maybe not for Hilda. What if something happened? Who'd care for Tiddles?

JULIA

Fair point. How about speed dating at the Woodman? She could meet someone who'd care for Tiddles if she can't. They're on Fridays, and we could do an Indian meal after.

JOAN

Speed dating? Hilda would be lost for words! And where would she put her shopping trolley?

JULIA

She could use my Gucci handbag instead—nobody ever says no to that!

JILL

You'd lend your Gucci? Could I borrow it for April's wedding in a few weeks?

JULIA

(Gasps)
Alright, I suppose so.

JOAN

Hilda doesn't eat curry anymore, though. She was into those Vesta curries in packets, but these days, she prefers Chinese.

(Phone rings. Joan stands scraping her chair and answers it, mumbling as she speaks.)

JULIA

What about a night out in the Chinese Quarter? We could get the train, have a meal, and then cocktails at the Alchemist.

(Joan returns to her seat with lots of chair shuffling noises.)

JILL

I like it. Or, we could just go to the Jade Wok in Solihull—might get a council discount. Cocktails could be at Turtle Bay nearby.

JOAN

But Hilda likes an early night. Tiddles doesn't like being left in the dark.

JULIA

She's quite the homebody, isn't she?

JOAN

Hilda used to be wild, actually and very glamorous. She worked as a croupier on cruise ships, loved gambling and drinking too much. Married the ship's captain, no less.

JULIA

Never! How did I not know?

JILL

Joan, how do you know all this?

JOAN

Seen the pictures and heard the stories of her all-night parties in the Caribbean. But everything fell apart when her husband, Geoff, fell overboard off St. Lucia. She was devastated.

JILL

Wait, who's Geoff?

JOAN

Her first love. He survived, but turned out to be married to someone else. Hilda came back to England, broken-hearted.

JILL

So, she never married the captain?

JOAN

Yes, Geoff was the captain.

JULIA

Did he get eaten by a shark or worse killed by a passing boat?

JOAN

Maybe he should have been for being a bigamist! He was rescued and airlifted to hospital where he stayed for several days with a crying Hilda by his side. Unfortunately, he'd failed to mention to Hilda that he already had a wife and when she turned up there was an ugly scene. Hilda was sent packing back to England and Geoff ended up in prison.

JILL

That's terrible! How could we have worked with Hilda for so long and not know her story?

JULIA

So that's why she never married. Is he still in prison?

JOAN

Geoff served his sentence and on his release tried to rekindle his relationship with his wife, but I heard they'd got divorced.

JILL

Let's get back to the leaving do! Are we going with Jade Wok for an early menu deal and then onto Turtle Bay for mocktails?

JOAN

Yes, why not! Although, she does love a quiz. Luck is her middle name and she wins everything!

JULIA

We all love a good quiz but it's too late to organise one now.

(The door opens. Hilda enters, dressed in a cream suit with a green hat. She carries Tiddles, who is wearing a matching bow. In her other arm is a box of Greggs cakes.)

JILL

Well, look who's here—and with a guest!

HILDA

Sorry I'm late! Let me just sign my visitor in and I'll be right back.

JOAN

Visitors aren't allowed in the basement.

JULIA

Come on, Joan, we can bend the rules this once. Go fetch your visitor, Hilda.

(Hilda exits briefly, shuffling feet heard fading and then she returns with an older gentleman, in a smart suit. They're holding hands.)

HILDA

Everyone, meet Geoff… my husband! We got married half an hour ago at the Solihull Registry office!

(Gasps from Jill, Joan, and Julia as Hilda beams, clutching Geoff's hand.)

JILL

Hold on! You never mentioned this before! Where did you meet? Why haven't you told us before? And how come you look so right together?

HILDA

Geoff's my first love. We've been seeing each other again for three months, and he proposed two weeks ago. I could write a book on our journey—maybe someday I will! But for now, I am happy and can't wait to leave work with Geoff by my side. A whole new life ahead of me.

(They all hug Hilda and Geoff. Tiddles meows and flexes her nails.)

JULIA

This is so romantic! Let's see the ring!

(Hilda proudly shows off her ring. Suitable aahs are heard.)

JILL

It's beautiful, very Princess Diana!

(Julia dashes to the stationery cupboard, grabs a handful of confetti, and throws it over Hilda, Geoff, and Tiddles, who starts sniffing and coughing.)

JULIA

Congratulations—you're a lovely couple.

HILDA

Thanks! Here are cakes and a bottle of Champagne to celebrate. But what are you lot doing sitting around the table?

JOAN

Planning your leaving do, of course! Although we might need to tweak our plans.

JULIA

Too right!

HILDA

Oh, I'm sorry but it's too late for that! We fly off to join the Black Princess straight after I finish work on Friday. But we've got tonight—let's celebrate! After cake, let's go out. I've got my bride's sash, unicorn balloons, and some china plates for a smashing Greek night at Zorba's with brandy and Irish coffees at the end. Who's in?

JOAN

I'm free!

JILL

Me too!

JULIA

Bring it on!

(Sound of a champagne cork popping and then Geoff passes around plastic cups.)

JILL

To the bride and groom!

EVERYONE

Cheers!

(Clinking glasses and slurps.)

JILL

Well, there's a turn-up for the books, we never saw that one coming!

(A couple of minutes later they are laughing as they gather their coats. The door slides open, and they head out into the sunlight.)

Hinge Gone Haywire

SIX MONTHS AGO, it felt like I had everything—an exciting relationship, a man who seemed to worship me, and a future that looked dazzling. We met on Hinge. I swiped right faster than you can say, 'Too good to be true.' Clive had it all: the looks, the charm, and the effortless way he seemed to know exactly what to say.

Looking back, maybe that was the first red flag. But who notices red flags when they're busy admiring perfect cheekbones?

Things started to change subtly. First, it was suggestions about my outfits. "Wear the blue dress tonight, darling. It brings out your eyes." Sweet, right? Then it was lingerie—lace, silk, straps I wasn't even sure how to get into. "Trust me, babe. You'll look like a goddess."

The filming started as a 'spontaneous' idea. "Just us, for fun," Clive had said, pulling out a tripod from a cupboard so quickly that I suspected he'd planned this for weeks. I laughed nervously, but he was persuasive. "You're gorgeous. Plus, I'll delete it straight after."

Spoiler: He didn't.

What came next was an avalanche of 'little things' that spiralled into something I barely recognised. Filming in daring locations? Sure, I could try that. Saying goodbye to nights out with friends? Well, they didn't really get us, did they? Somewhere between the endless 'requests' and the expensive dinners I somehow ended up paying for, I realised Clive wasn't the dream I thought he was.

The night it all came crashing down, he insisted on taking me to Sinbars—a dodgy 'exclusive' club that his mate owned. "You'll love it," he said, flashing that dazzling grin. "It's classy."

It wasn't.

The place smelled like weed and regret, with corners draped in black satin and people hovering with cameras like vultures waiting for fresh prey. I clung to Clive's arm, whispering, "Can we go?"

"Relax, sweetheart. Just one drink."

Before I knew it, I was seated on one of the beds, awkwardly sipping a cocktail named something ridiculous like 'Sultry Sin.' Clive sauntered off to chat with the bartender, leaving me to fend off someone trying to convince me to 'join in the fun.' Fun? If Clive thought this was a date night, we clearly had different definitions of romance.

When I snapped and said I wanted to leave, Clive waved me off. "Sure, babe, take a cab. I'll catch up later."

Later never came.

Back at my flat, still fuming, I opened the app a friend had recommended—a spy camera detector. I'd downloaded it as a joke. Imagine my surprise when five blinking lights popped up in my bedroom.

For a moment, I was stunned. Then, I grabbed a chair, stood on it, and yanked down the first hidden camera. "Really, Clive?" I muttered. "Spy cameras? I'm not that interesting."

The cameras went into a shoebox destined for the recycling bin. Before pulling the last one off the curtain rod, I flipped it the bird and said, “Goodbye, Clive. Don’t call me. Actually, do—so I can ignore it.”

I slept like a baby that night. For the first time in months, I felt free.

Leap Year 2024

IN THE LEAD-UP to Christmas that year, the house buzzed with whispered conversations and laughter. Mum—the hardworking matriarch of the otherwise chaotic family—had polished the wooden floor until it gleamed, filling the air with the scent of beeswax. Even Rusty, the family's ever-energetic Jack Russell, was on his best behaviour, a rare feat for such a seasoned escape artist.

Susanne, the eldest sibling, looked immaculate. Her nails were freshly manicured, and she wore a new high-necked red mini dress that skimmed her hips, making her dark, shoulder-length bob shine. Poised and self-assured, she'd hinted all week that today would be a memorable one.

The family, dressed in their Sunday best and gathered in the lounge, anticipation building as they waited for a knock at the door. The room glowed with festive charm, with paper chains catching the light from the Christmas tree, casting shimmering reflections across the walls. Carols played softly, glasses of Champagne stood ready, and a 'special' cake sat in a tin in the kitchen.

At last, a knock sounded. Susanne sprang up to answer, while everyone else clambered onto the green leather sofas, eyes gleaming with expectation. As Tim entered, all eyes turned to Susanne's carefully wrapped present.

"Don't keep us waiting, Susanne!" Mum urged, smiling, her hands still soapy from last-minute washing up.

Dad hushed her with a finger to his lips. "Let's sit down and let her open it. I'll wash up later."

Tim shifted uncomfortably, glancing around the room. "So, what did everyone get for Christmas?"

"Oh, I got Buckaroo," Julie, Susanne's younger sister replied, tugging her jumper down over her knees. "But I wanted Cluedo!"

"Stop pulling at your jumper," Mum chided. "You'll stretch it out of shape, and I keep telling you… Cluedo was sold out!"

Susanne's brother, Ivan, shrugged. "I got Action Man," he muttered, tossing it at Tim.

"Careful, Ivan, that nearly fell on the floor!" Mum scolded. "Honestly, all of you, show some gratitude. Ignore them, Tim."

Mum turned to Susanne with a soft smile as she sat down next to Dad. "So, what's your present, love?"

Susanne, eyes bright, tore into the wrapping paper, revealing a plain cardboard box. Opening it, she pulled out a hollow black plastic tube, blinking in confusion.

Laughing (rather hysterically), she blew into the tube as if it were a toy. "What a great surprise," she joked, setting it down. "Now, where's my real present?"

Rusty, seizing his moment, bounded forward, snatched the tube, and dashed around the room, to everyone's amusement. Only Tim looked tense, glancing at the floor.

"Drop it, Rusty!" Dad shouted, standing up and pointing toward the door. Obediently, Rusty dropped the tube and trotted out of the lounge, head and tail low, Dad followed him out.

Susanne put her hand over her mouth and tried to be serious and bent down to pick it up. "Wow, it's… different!"

The siblings exchanged amused looks, playing along. "Yes, fabulous! But, er… what is it?" said Julie.

"Can I shoot peas through it?" asked Ivan.

Susanne pulled out the rest of the box's contents, her amusement fading. Tears pricked her eyes as she looked at Tim. "It's… not quite what I anticipated." Putting her full attention at an imaginary bit of fluff on her dress she mumbled, "Well this is one present I'll never forget."

Tim, his voice trembling, explained, "It's a tube to water the roots of the magnolia tree you've always wanted." He smiled weakly. "You keep saying you can't keep plants alive. I was planning to install it… along with a magnolia tree." Taking in everyone's face he searched for an ally. There were none. He pulled at his collar around a neck that had gone bright red and wondered how quickly he could make his exit.

Susanne composed herself, dabbing her eyes she reminded herself how much she loved him. "Well, it's certainly… different." She sighed. "After eight years together, not quite the present I expected though."

Rubbing a shoe on the carpet, Tim shoved his hands in his pockets. "Maybe I should go," he murmured, rising to his feet.

Susanne managed a shaky smile, watching him leave, before bolting upstairs, her tears falling freely. Moments later, the sound of Tim's car engine drifted away.

Mum, trying to lighten the atmosphere, stood up, "Julie, why don't you make us some tea and bring in the biscuits?"

Julie hurried to the kitchen, stashing the 'special' cake tin on the top shelf of the larder, thinking, Next year, maybe…

29th February 2024

Susanne had been quiet lately, but her eyes betrayed a flicker of hope. That morning, the doorbell rang, and Julie answered it, finding a florist's delivery.

"Flowers for Susanne," the florist said, handing over a stunning bouquet of twelve red roses.

Susanne was still in bed, so Julie rushed upstairs with them.

"Oh my God, they're gorgeous!" Susanne laughed as she tore open the envelope to read the card. "They're from Tim, he's written 'All my love.'"

"Where's he taking you tonight?" Julie asked, bouncing with excitement.

"To the Stage Coach in Highgrove. It's a quaint Victorian place and I hear it is very romantic."

"Wow, sounds divine! Do you think he'll pop the question?"

Susanne sighed. "Not likely."

When Tim arrived at seven-thirty sharp, the family couldn't help but admire how lovely they looked together. Susanne wore a floor-length turquoise dress with her hair styled in an elegant chignon, her nails perfectly matched to her dress. Tim was in a sharp dark blue suit, accented with the turquoise tie Susanne had bought him.

"Have a wonderful time!" Mum called as they left.

"Need a lift into town?" Dad offered.

"All sorted," Tim replied with a kind smile.

Once they'd gone, the family group chat buzzed with updates:

Susanne: "Everything's going to plan. The restaurant has it, and the timing should be perfect."

Julie: "Fingers crossed!"

Susanne: "Tim seems a bit nervous tonight. Keeps checking his pockets."

Julie: "Don't worry!"

Susanne: "He's ordered Champagne and two glasses!"

Julie: "Bloody hell, what's going on?!"

Susanne: "I tried to stop the restaurant from bringing out the 'special surprise'... Too late. They brought it while I was in the ladies' room. I'm scared to go back to the table!"

Julie: "Just brazen it out."

Moments later, a video pinged into the family's WhatsApp group. It showed Tim, down on one knee, proposing to Susanne, ring in a box. And Susanne sitting on a Black and Decker Workmate holding a sign that said, 'Will you marry me?'

The family responded with cheers, glasses clinking and the 'special' engagement cake cut in Susanne's honour. They laughed, celebrating the double proposal.

Someone shouted, "Well, Tim's always wanted a Black and Decker Workmate!"

Unplugged

THE HAPPY HEART Café buzzed with noise, the clatter of cups, and the rich aroma of freshly brewed coffee and sticky treats. Emily Pankhurst-White scanned the room for a free table. The only option was in the corner, cluttered with crockery and crumbs. Sighing, she stacked the used plates and mugs onto a tray and waited until a waitress appeared to wipe the table clean.

The waitress pulled a notepad from her apron. "It's busy today. What can I get you?"

"A small latte, extra hot, and a cinnamon swirl, please," Emily replied, offering a broad smile.

The waitress paused, curious. "What's that you're scribbling?"

"Just my notes. I'm a comedian," Emily explained, tapping her pen on the page.

"Really? Are you famous?"

Emily shook her head. "Sadly, no. But I've been on TV and even had a book of jokes published." She reached into her backpack and handed the waitress a slim book.

The waitress's eyes widened as she read the cover. "So, you're Emily Pankhurst-White!" She grinned. "Refreshments are on the house. You're on in twenty minutes, and there's already quite a crowd." Noticing Emily's chewed nails she added, "Are you nervous?"

Emily shifted in her seat, hiding her hands in her pockets. “Thanks. I haven’t done a gig in ages. I’m a bit shy actually.”

The waitress patted her arm. “You’ll be great. I’ll bring your coffee and cake over.”

Emily sat back, enjoying the atmosphere and observing the room. People-watching was a guilty pleasure, and this café was the perfect setting. At the front, Pam, loud and obnoxious, held court among a group of women who hung on her every word. Emily recognised her—overconfident, attention-seeking. Pam would be trouble; she’d need to be taken down a peg or two.

When the coffee arrived, Emily took a deep sip, letting the warmth calm her nerves. It had been years since she’d performed, but she still had it in her. She just needed to focus. Forget the chaos at home—Henry could deal with that mess. He’d caused it, after all.

When the time came, she stood and walked to the stage. Applause rippled through the room as she began her act.

“So, Angela,” she said, pointing to the ringleader in the front row, “what made you come here today?”

“Nothing on telly, to be honest,” the woman replied with a smirk. “And my name’s Pam. Do you know me? You look familiar.”

Emily grinned. “Oh, I know people like you.” She pulled a face, eliciting laughter from the crowd. Pam frowned, clearly racking her brain.

Emily laughed inwardly. Pam had never been sharp.

As the set progressed, Emily had the audience eating out of her hand, weaving Pam into her jokes until the woman squirmed in her seat. Pam still hadn't figured out how they knew each other. Emily, with her blonde hair, blue eyes, and slimmed-down figure, looked entirely different these days. Contact lenses and a few lost pounds had done wonders.

During the interval, Henry slipped in and took a seat at the back. He was Emily's greatest fan. Flashy in his new clothes, he caught Emily's eye. She signalled subtly, nodding towards Pam. Henry adjusted his cap and turned up his collar. Emily smiled; he fancied himself a spy.

By the second half, Emily was in her element. Her jokes grew edgier, and her gaze locked onto Pam.

"What do you call a nurse who turns off the life-support machine?" she quipped.

"Stupid!" someone shouted.

"Energy efficient!" another chimed in.

Pam shot out of her seat, heading for the door. Emily's voice rang out, stopping her. "A murderer! Someone who doesn't deserve to live. What do you say, Pam?"

Pam turned, her face twisted in fury. "I know who you are now, Emily. You're a real piece of work." Her voice shook with contempt. "Seven years in that hellhole prison while your twin sister and my husband's affair caused the crash that killed them both. I didn't turn off the machine, but I wish I had. At least then I'd have earned my fate—losing my career, my children, and my home."

Emily clapped slowly, her smile icy. "Good story, Pam. But why not be honest and tell the truth?"

Pam folded her arms and glared at Emily. "It wasn't me who turned off the machine—it was a man. Funny how they never caught him, isn't it?"

The room fell silent, and Pam stormed out, slamming the door behind her.

Later, Henry and Emily stopped for a celebratory drink. When they returned home and opened the door, a vile smell of death hit them as soon as they stepped into the kitchen.

"What's that stench?" Emily asked, wrinkling her nose. "Where's it coming from?"

Henry's smirk was almost gleeful. "The utility room. Someone took the tape off the plug and switched off the freezer. That wouldn't have been you, would it?"

Emily froze. "I… I didn't mean to…"

Henry leaned in, his eyes glittering with menace. "Careless, Emily. Very careless."

Her stomach churned as she realised her next words might be her last.

Hey! Maracanã—Dancing in the Rain

Leaving Rio

Leaving was bittersweet. It might well have been our last visit to South America.

We'd had an incredible time, ticking off the must-see sights: Copacabana Beach, Christ the Redeemer, Sugar Loaf Mountain, and the Lapa Steps—where Snoop Dogg filmed his music video for Beautiful. During the day, we strolled the streets soaking up the city's vibrancy. And in the evenings, we indulged in Caipirinha cocktails and the fabulous local cuisine at various bars and restaurants.

The most challenging experience for me was Sugar Loaf Mountain. My fear of heights made it no easy feat.

Rob, ever the patient one, stood directly in front of me as we boarded the cable car. "Don't look down. Just keep your eyes on me. It's only a four-minute ride."

I gripped the handrail with clammy hands. "What if one of the cables snaps?"

"That's never happened. Honestly, it's safe," he reassured me with a calm smile.

Thankfully, the day was still, and the cable car didn't sway at all.

Another traveller, Patrick, joined us for some of the sights. He seemed overly cautious, always looking over his shoulder and staying close to us. Eventually, he shared why.

"I met someone from my hotel last week," he began, glancing around nervously. "He went for a walk alone one night."

"They always warn against that," I said. "I hope he wasn't wearing labels or jewellery."

"He wasn't," Patrick said quietly.

"What happened?" Rob asked, his voice gentle.

Patrick hesitated, his eyes scanning the mountain as though expecting danger. Then he continued, his voice barely above a whisper, "He was attacked by a group of men. They beat him up and stripped him of everything—his clothes, wallet, phone. Left him completely naked."

I stared at Patrick, waiting for a punch line that never came. The sadness in his eyes told me he wasn't joking.

"They left him there?" I asked.

"He woke up on the pavement, covered in blood. No one helped him. He had to find his way back to his hotel on his own."

I reached out and held Patrick's hand, feeling his body tremble. Eventually, he calmed, his hot, clammy hands turning cold. We never spoke of it again, but I hoped his holiday improved and that he never ventured out alone after dark.

The Semi-Final Football Match

Sometimes, you're just in the right place at the right time. For us, it was the Semi-Final football match—Fluminense vs Flamengo—on 9th March 2024.

Our bus was meant to pick us up at 6 pm, but, in true Brazilian fashion, it turned up over forty-five minutes late. The driver and guide were lively, handing out tickets and stopping at a petrol station so we could buy team strips. As we were seated in the family stands, it didn't matter which team's colours we chose.

"When are the strips arriving?" someone asked.

"They're on their way now," the guide replied.

Eventually, they arrived, and just as we bought them, the heavens opened. Ponchos were hastily purchased before we set off on foot to the Maracanã Stadium, following the guide through streets filled with the smells of food and the sounds of laughter and excitement.

Inside the stadium, the atmosphere was electric. The Brazilian passion for football was on full display, and even as a casual fan, I was swept up in the energy. Massive flags waved, thunder and lightning cracked across the sky, and fireworks added to the spectacle.

We stood for the entire match, shouting and cheering alongside the locals. Their enthusiasm was infectious, and by the time the Flamengo team claimed victory, I was hugging Rob and laughing.

"Why are the Fluminense fans leaving already?" I asked.

Rob grinned. "They know it's over and want to beat the traffic."

"More fool them!" I said, grabbing his hand and twirling into a clumsy tango.

As the game ended, fireworks competed with the storm overhead. We joined the crowds streaming out of the stadium, singing along with Brazilian fans and feeling completely safe in the jubilant atmosphere.

Back on the bus, we sang *Oh, What a Night* at full volume, waving to our new friends as we left behind an unforgettable evening.

The Day We Left

My heart was heavy as we headed for Rio International Airport. As we checked out of our hotel, I couldn't shake the feeling that this might be the last time we'd see South America.

We checked in and dropped off our suitcases and then made our way through security. With the metal in Rob's hip, security was always a bit of a hassle. I'd never had any problems—until now.

The scanner beeped as I walked through, and a guard gestured for me to step aside. She called over a colleague, who ran a handheld scanner over me.

"Metal in the leg?" she asked in heavily accented English.

"No," I replied, baffled.

I took off my trainers, which they whisked away. The scanner beeped again as they ran it over my body.

"Metal in the leg?" the guard repeated, her tone now laced with impatience.

"No," I said, my face flushing with embarrassment. I briefly saw Rob in the distance and he motioned that he would take care of my stuff.

They led me into a small room, locked the door, and pulled on gloves. One of them lifted my top and ran the scanner closer to my skin.

I felt hot and flustered, unsure of what they were searching for. I wished I could understand them. I felt like a criminal and just did as they indicated.

I briefly wondered if I should say yes and then they might let me go, but I thought better of it.

They motioned to my waist and I moved the band of my leggings down. The scanner made a noise, but they could see nothing was there. They whispered to each other then turned back to me.

"Metal in the leg?" the guard asked again, clearly frustrated.

"No," I said for what felt like the hundredth time. Then, a thought struck me.

Reaching down, I tugged at the small metal tag stitched into the side of my jumper. "Could it be this?" I asked.

The guards exchanged a look before hurrying me out of the room. They returned my trainers and waved me over to a chair. Rob rushed to my side, handing me my belongings.

“What happened?” he asked.

“It was awful,” I said, tears streaming down my face. “I had no idea what was going on. I felt like a criminal.”

“We can leave now,” he said, putting an arm around me.

“Not yet,” I replied, steering us towards a chemist.

“Why are we going there?”

“To buy nail scissors,” I said firmly. “That label is coming off—I’m not going through that again!”

An Easter Encounter

TODAY IS MY SPECIAL day. There's a flurry of secretive phone calls happening downstairs, my hair has been styled into soft waves, and a posh dress hangs neatly on the wardrobe door. I pretend not to notice, but the truth is, I know exactly what's going on—there's a surprise birthday party being planned for me.

The Post Arrives

The doorbell chimes, and I find a battered brown parcel sitting on the step. It's clearly been through a rough journey, the edges scuffed and the tape barely holding it together. I rarely get anything in the post, so I'm surprised to find my name and address scribbled across the front. The sender remains a mystery.

I frown, lifting it carefully. "Who on earth could this be from?"

Mum appears at the doorway, wiping her hands on a tea towel. "What is it?"

"No idea. I'm not expecting anything. It looks like it's come from Ireland."

Her eyes narrow in curiosity. "Southern Ireland? That's where your dad's family is from, isn't it? You'd best open it."

I place the box on the kitchen counter, hesitant. "Later, maybe. I'll wait for now."

Mum's jaw tightens, and she fixes me with a look. "Well, it's your choice," she mutters before stomping upstairs and slamming her bedroom door.

Shrugging, not understanding what was bothering Mum, I turn on the TV, losing myself in the madness of Jeremy Kyle. The stories seem to escalate with every guest—a baby on cocaine, a secret sibling appearing for a DNA test, and a woman desperately defending herself against accusations of infidelity. The drama is grim but addictive.

Eventually, my gaze drifts back to the parcel. A sticker reads Gift – Handle with Care. A faint return address catches my eye: Ashford Solicitor, on behalf of Mr and Mrs J Long, High Street, Dun Laoghaire.

A wave of confusion washes over me, they both died years ago. "Mum!" I shout upstairs. "It's from Attracta and John's solicitor."

The sound of hurried footsteps follows. Mum reappears, her curiosity now piqued. "Attracta and John? My sister and her husband? But they've been dead for years. What on earth could it be?"

I grab a pair of scissors and carefully cut through the tape. Mum leans in, both of us holding our breath. Inside, nestled in layers of straw, is something astonishing—a Fabergé egg, gleaming in the sunlight.

Mum gasps, covering her mouth. "Oh, my goodness! That's their limited-edition egg. Attracta always called it their child. It sat in pride of place in their lounge."

Her voice trembles as she reaches out to touch it. "Eighteen-carat yellow gold, Blue John stone, diamonds… even the pedestal is carved from Blue John. She told me once it was hand-designed, completely unique. Attracta always had expensive taste."

I'm in awe. "Why would they send it to me, though? I'm one of five kids."

"There must be a letter," Mum murmurs, rummaging through the straw. Sure enough, a neatly folded envelope appears. It's addressed to me.

Hands trembling, I open it and begin to read:

> Dear Jill,
>
> Happy twenty-first birthday!
>
> We hope you cherish the egg as much as we did. It was the child we always longed for, so we wanted to ensure it went to a good home. We remember how carefully you held it years ago and how fascinated you were by its story. Before we passed, we made arrangements with our solicitor to send this to you when you came of age.
>
> We want to leave you with something special, to remind you of our love even though we only got to know you as a teenager. Use it however you see fit—keep it, sell it, or use the money for a deposit on your first home. Whatever you choose, we'll be smiling down on you today, on your very special celebration.
>
> Love you to the moon and back.
>
> Yours always,
>
> Attracta and John xx

Tears prick my eyes as I finish reading. "But why me?" I ask, my voice breaking. "Why not one of the others? And why would she put love you to the moon on a letter to me?"

Mum hesitates, her face pale. She looks away, fiddling with her hands. "There's something I need to tell you, Jill."

I stare at her, dread rising in my chest. "What?"

Taking a deep breath, she meets my eyes. "The year you were born, Attracta came to England. She stayed with us for several months to recover… after you were born."

The air leaves the room. "Are you saying…?"

Mum nods, her expression unreadable. "I never wanted you to know. Trust Attracta to have the last word—and use that damned egg to do it."

The Hidden Room

The Apartment in Pollensa

BUYING A HOLIDAY home in Old Town Pollensa, Mallorca, with its winding streets, shutters, and roof terraces, had always seemed like an impossible dream. We viewed several properties, but the moment we saw the stone house near the church, we were captivated. Even before the estate agent opened the door, we knew it was the one. It felt like a dream come true.

The house was split into two apartments. On the ground floor, there were three good-sized bedrooms, an oversized lounge with a high red-brick Spanish fireplace, a small kitchen, and a large, out-dated brown bathroom suite. The layout needed updating, but it had potential. The only drawback was the shared internal porch entrance and the staircase leading to the upstairs apartment. Books and tins of food were strewn across the steps, making me wonder how the upstairs owners even managed to climb them. The estate agent assured us they were rarely there, but I couldn't shake the thought of potential nuisances.

Outside, the cobbled street leading to the house became slippery when it rained, which made me worry about visitors navigating the famous Calvari Steps in winter. Yet, the rooftop terrace made up for everything. The view of the Tramontana Mountains was breath-taking. Sheep and goats grazed below, and the uninterrupted scenery felt magical.

Inside, the rooms needed modernising, from a complete electrical refit to installing air-conditioning units. Large swirls adorned the ceilings, which Rob declared had to go.

"These swirls remind me of the Artex in every room on Bamley Road," he said, shaking his head.

"Thank goodness you said that!" I replied. "The kitchen and bathroom are dreadful, but the views make up for it. And the price is a steal with no damp problems and so much potential."

"Let's get a builder to quote for the renovations and then put an offer in," Rob said, taking copious notes. I couldn't wait to make the house our own. In my head, I was already rearranging furniture and deciding which rooms to tackle first.

The builder gave a glowing report about the apartment. He inspired me with confidence and promised to send a quote within the next few days. He would start the renovations once the property was ours.

It's Ours!

The day we collected the keys, I danced up the cobbled street to our new home. The previous owners, a German couple, had left all the furniture, which wasn't unusual in Spain. The scent of pine trees and freshly baked pretzels lingered in the air, as though they'd arranged a farewell gesture.

That evening, we spent hours cleaning and organising. By bedtime, we felt at home, though the builders were due to start knocking down walls the following week.

As we drifted off to sleep, Rob suddenly sat up.

"What's that noise?" he whispered. "It sounds like tapping, coming from inside the apartment."

I listened closely. "I can hear it too. It's faint, it reminds me of tap dancing."

"No one's arrived at the upstairs apartment," Rob said. "I wonder where it's coming from."

"That's a question for tomorrow. Let's get some sleep."

Neighbours and Noise

The next day, we introduced ourselves to a neighbour.

"Hola, encantado de conocerte. Somos Rob y Jill. Nos hemos mudado al apartamento de al lado en la planta baja," Rob said confidently.

The woman, Edna, smiled warmly. "Bienvenido. Me llamo Edna Brown, y he vivido aquí 36 años."

Rob explained to me that her name was Edna Brown. I smiled and said, "Hola!" which was the extent of my Spanish.

"You've got a very English name," Rob remarked.

Edna laughed. "I was born in Bath but moved here as a child. I can speak English if you prefer."

"That would be great," Rob said.

As we chatted, Edna told us about the Tiago family, who had owned the upstairs apartment. "They left for Palma three years ago."

"That's odd," I said. "We keep hearing noises a bit like tap dancing coming from upstairs."

Edna looked puzzled. “Their daughter, Lucy, was a dancer—ballet, tap, ballroom—but she left with them. They never sold the apartment. Strange family.”

“I wonder why they never sold the apartment,” said Rob.

Edna shook her head. “It is a mystery. I know it is in a bad state of repair.”

“Did you ever meet the German family who lived in our apartment?” I asked.

“No, though I heard they couldn’t settle here and they were standoffish with the locals.”

“Do you know if the Tiagos left a forwarding address in Palma?” I asked.

Edna blinked and didn’t speak for some time, her face taking on a grave expression. Then she shook her head. “No, they just left without saying a word. It now seems odd as we were very friendly at the time. I must go now as I have to cook lunch for Tirso.”

As she climbed the steps, she kept shaking her head and we heard her muttering to herself.

The conversation left us more confused than ever. The tapping noises persisted, becoming an eerie part of our nights.

The Builders Uncover a Secret

When the builders arrived, they got straight to work. Jordi, their foreman, greeted me warmly. "Good morning, Mrs G… sorry, Jill. We'll cover the furniture and start on the kitchen wall. By the way, this is Miguel, so you know… his English is not so good."

Miguel smiled and nodded at the mention of his name.

Rob and I stayed out of their way, scraping wallpaper in the bedrooms while they set to work knocking the kitchen wall down. After not very long, Miguel points out the dust.

"That's a sign for tea, am I right?"

"Too right, Jill," laughed Jordi.

Mid-morning, Jordi called us into the kitchen. "There's a false wall here." He pointed to a corner. "Shall we knock through?" We nod, instantly curious about the prospect of a secret room. Miguel wasted no time hammering through it. Dust filled the air as weak mortar crumbled away, revealing a hidden space.

Clapping in excitement I have to stop myself from jumping up and down. "It's the size of a room!"

Sunlight floods in. Inside the cavity lay cobwebs, a pair of ballet and tap shoes, and something pink wrapped in plastic. Rob and I stepped closer, prodding the bundle with our scrapers.

"Oh my God!" I gasped.

"What is it?" Jordi asked.

"It's a skeleton."

The sight was chilling. A young girl's remains lay in the corner, dressed in a pink tutu with jeans. Shoes and medals were scattered around her. Jordi crossed himself, while Miguel pulled out his rosary beads and began to pray loudly.

Rob and I make the sign of the cross and request a two-minute silence.

"It looks like a young girl," said Jordi. "What an end to a young life." He shook his head with tear-filled eyes.

Rob called the police, who arrived swiftly. They photographed the scene and removed the remains, speculating that the victim was a young girl. Telling us they would check dental records. I mentioned the tapping noises we'd heard, wondering if they were connected to her restless spirit.

Jordi kept crossing himself and muttering about the poor soul trying to be found.

The police told us we needed to leave the apartment as it was now their crime scene. It would be two weeks before we could move back in, and I spent the whole time trying to work out the tragic tale.

Piecing Together the Mystery

Over the following weeks, the police investigated. The Tiagos, who were still paying taxes on the upstairs apartment, denied any knowledge of the skeleton. DNA tests confirmed the remains didn't match their family.

Despite the removal of the body, which I had assumed was the cause of our haunting, the tapping noise continued and I often woke at night to hear it.

Then, during further renovations, Jordi discovered a piece of paper hidden in the plaster. It bore the name Anna. When they were contacted about it, the German couple revealed that Edna's husband, Tirso, had installed the fireplace years ago and that he had a daughter named Anna, who was known for her rebellious streak.

When confronted, Edna and Tirso admitted to a tragic accident. They had hidden Anna's body out of fear and shame. The police arrested them, and the case was closed.

But for the townspeople of Pollensa, it was only the beginning. Café chatter buzzed with theories, as every neighbour claimed to have "always suspected something." The market stalls became stages for impromptu re-enactments of Tirso's stoic denial or Edna's trembling confession. Tourists, curious and morbid, flocked to the house, snapping pictures and whispering about 'the room.'

For weeks, Pollensa had its own soap opera, with Edna and Tirso at the centre. Even as the town returned to its tranquil rhythm, their story lingered like a shadow cast on the cobbled streets—an eerie reminder that secrets never stay buried for long.

Gratitude ran through us when the gossip began to wane.

The tapping noises ceased from the day of the arrest, and a sense of peace settled over the apartment. Though the discovery had shaken us, we were determined to make the house a home, honouring its past while looking forward to the future.

And when Jordi suggested knocking through to our rooftop terrace, we ever so politely declined.

Beautiful Betsy

I NEVER EXPECTED to land a job in Communication and Implementation, especially as five candidates were in the running, including two already in the department. Part of the role involved analysing Mapper Software before it was uploaded to the system, which was challenging but intriguing. The interview process was intense and included case-based reasoning tests, which I surprisingly enjoyed.

Once hired, I joined a small team of two, handling help desk operations for the entire site. Our duties included ensuring that timesheets from contracted programmers were accurate and input into the system correctly, as well as safeguarding the network's security. Month-end work, with its bills, invoices, and salary runs, often meant long hours.

The only personal downside was not being allowed my mobile phone in the office. With three kids at three different schools, it was inconvenient when the schools needed to contact me. Unless they rang the office directly, I wouldn't know if something happened.

I shared a small, glass-walled office—fondly nicknamed the fishbowl—with my colleague, Betsy. In her fifties, she was slim, with striking bright red hair and an impeccable sense of style. Funny and exceptionally skilled at her job, Betsy inspired awe in me; she seemed to handle everything effortlessly.

During my first week, I noticed a peculiar pattern: several calls came in each day, where the caller would hang up as soon as I answered. Frustrated, I complained to Betsy, disappointed that the caller didn't want to speak to me.

"Don't worry," she said, smiling kindly. "It's probably just a wrong number. I can take calls at that time if you'd prefer."

"No, but thank you. I'd rather take them—just in case one's from one of the schools about the kids."

Still, the calls continued. I began to wonder if it was because I was new or if the callers preferred speaking to Betsy, who had years of experience. As weeks turned into months, the situation became unbearable.

"This is ridiculous, Betsy," I vented one afternoon. "Same time every day, same nonsense. I won't stand for it anymore."

She apologised for the inconvenience, assured me I was doing a great job, and then reapplied her lipstick, adjusted her hair, spritzed perfume, and left the office. This routine became a regular occurrence.

I asked in the programmers' office about it and noticed everyone smirk and share an amused look, but I was told not to worry as it had nothing to do with my job. When Betsy returned to the office, she carried an air of mystery about her and I never had the courage to confront her about it.

I couldn't shake the feeling that something strange was going on. One day, after another silent call, I snapped. "If you're going to call, at least have the decency to speak! Stop wasting my time."

Betsy's face turned ashen. "What have you done?"

"What do you mean? Nothing!"

She quickly left the office and was gone for hours. Surprisingly, the calls stopped… for a few days.

Later, I mentioned the incident to a programmer next door.

"I think you've made a mistake," one of them said cryptically. "Just leave it alone—it's nothing to do with your work, and you don't want to stir up trouble."

I returned to the office, unsure what to make of it. Betsy was getting ready to leave, her usual perfume and lipstick routine in place. "If anyone calls tell them I am on site visiting a client."

"Can I have a contact number, just in case?"

"I'll check in, I will only be in the other building," she replied, looking slightly sheepish.

"Thanks Betsy, that's appreciated, especially as it's month end with lots going on."

"I will be with Patrick Sutton sorting out salaries. I am hopeful we can input the revised data before we initiate the run today."

"Okay, I will schedule that run for later today."

The mystery of the calls remained unsolved, though my paranoia subsided somewhat. I convinced myself it was simply a preference for speaking with Betsy.

Finding the Truth

I decided to say no more and neither did Betsy. We occasionally received the odd intermittent call but most calls now went to her mobile. She received a dispensation, to bring her mobile phone into the office.

I mulled over the conversation I had with the programmers some time before. They thought there was more to it and said it had nothing to do with my work.

But I couldn't let it go entirely. One morning, I decided to visit Faith, the switchboard supervisor.

"Hi, Faith," I greeted her and her team, Heather and Cassie. "Busy as always?"

"You know it! What brings you here?"

"I wanted to ask if you've noticed anything odd. For months, I'd get calls that disconnected as soon as I answered. It stopped after I had words with the caller, but it was driving me mad."

Faith froze. "Oh no. Tell me you didn't say anything!"

"I might've lost my temper…"

She exchanged a panicked look with her colleagues. "You can't breathe a word of this, Jill. Promise us."

"Of course," I said, even more curious now.

"It's the Head of Site, Paul Murton."

I felt the blood drain from my face. I remembered seeing him recently, red-faced and visibly furious. Now I knew why.

I couldn't confront him—or even acknowledge the situation. My job depended on staying silent!

Can I See?

JORDAN'S GRIP ON MY ARM was sudden, vice-like. I staggered, breath-catching, tumbling into my worst nightmare.

He yanked the wardrobe door open. "Get in there, be quiet, and don't move. I'll let you out when I get back from work." His shower-wet hair dripped onto the floor, each drop echoing in the silence.

I stared at the growing puddle at his feet, my body trembling. Any protest, any sign of defiance, would make things worse. His punishments had grown more creative lately, and the thought of what might come next froze me. My breath quickened, uneven, and my heart hammered my ribs. The darkness ahead swallowed me whole as he shoved me inside. The wardrobe doors closed with a dull click, followed by the unmistakable sound of the key turning in the lock.

Minutes later, the front door slammed. The car engine revved, tyres crunching on the gravel outside. Silence.

I wept uncontrollably, eyes fixed on the thin cracks of light under the doors, each one mocking me. In the cramped darkness, I curled into myself, my bruised skin scraping against the sharp edges of hangers and shoes. My fingers trembled as they brushed over the familiar shapes of my leather handbags, now useless relics in this prison.

The silence pressed in on me, suffocating. A ticking time bomb; not the pain, nor the darkness, or even the confined space—injustice made me explode. I screamed, over and over, desperate for someone to hear. But no one would. No one ever heard me scream in our delectable detached Victorian. Only Jordan, my soul mate turned tormentor.

Time slipped by in jagged fragments. My thoughts spiralled. He wouldn't leave me here, would he? This was a trick. He'd come back, laughing, teasing me for being so scared. But as the seconds stretched into minutes, reality hit me like a slap. He'd left me. He wasn't coming back until he decided he was ready. Panic took over and I hammered the door until my hands were too bruised to continue.

With my head in my hands, wild thoughts dragged me down into a pit of despair. Clawing my way out of it, I resumed my attack on our made-to-measure wardrobe doors with my feet this time.

Each jerk caused pain to shoot through me. Ten minutes of fruitless kicking sent me into sobs of self-pity. Where's Ted? Frantic for comfort, I tore at the shoe boxes but when I couldn't find him, I put my head back and howled.

Time elapsed, I didn't know how much but it dawned on me that this was no trick; Jordan wasn't coming to let me out until he returned from work. What if he doesn't come home? Terror, raw and dreadful consumed me as I imagined myself becoming a skeleton in my perfect bedroom fittings.

I needed to concentrate and think of a way to get out. But how? My breath came in ragged gasps and sweat dripped down my back though my hands were freezing. My mind raced, searching for something—anything.

My phone! Maybe it was still on the bedside table.

Fearing the monster was waiting downstairs to torment me, I mumbled, "Alexa, call Mum." The faint cry for help got swallowed up in the thick silence of the empty house.

Nothing happened. No AI response, no ringtone, and no steps running up the stairs. Jordan had gone. If he was still here, he'd already be gloating, standing outside the wardrobe mocking me. I put my mouth close to the door and shouted. "Alexa, call Mum!"

The ringing tone broke the silence, sharp and sudden. My heart skipped a beat and started racing.

"Hello, Darling. Lovely to hear from you," Mum's voice floated through the air.

Tears streamed down my face as I cried into the darkness, "Help me, Mum. Please."

"Lucy? What's wrong? Are you okay?" Her voice grew louder, panicked. "Where are you? I can't hear you, speak up!"

"I'm locked in the wardrobe," I choked out, sobbing. "Can you get me out?" I yelled with a bit more force.

"I'm on my way. Hang in there, you're a brave girl. I love you."

Minutes felt like hours as I waited, curled into a ball, listening for the sound of her car. I nearly passed out from relief when I heard the front door unlock, and then her footsteps, heavy and urgent, racing up the stairs.

"Lucy, are you in there?"

I heard the panic in her voice. "Yes, but I'm scared, Mum. Hurry, he could come back any second."

Her voice grew sharper, angrier. "Has that bastard taken the key?"

I whimpered, my words choking me. "I think so. He took it out and I didn't hear him put it down." My hands shook, counting in my head, trying to block out the darkness. One, two, three, four... I repeated over and over like a prayer—my attempt to block the terror of the confined space.

"Stay with me, Lucy. I'll use his baseball bat. Does he still keep it under the bed?"

"Yes, hurry, Mummy." The sounds of Mum shuffling around didn't ease my palpitations. Shrinking back into the corner I put my head on my knees and covered it with my hands.

The first crack of the bat against the door knob made me jump. The door rattled with each of Mum's mighty blows. The door handle crashed to the floor on the twentieth whack. Mum yanked the door open and light poured in causing me to blink at the sudden brightness.

Mum stood there, panting, bat in hand, sweat rolling down her face. She looked like my personal superhero.

She pulled me out, and I collapsed into her arms, her familiar scent wrapping around me like a safety blanket. My body shook with sobs as words tumbled from my mouth, each one a bullet tearing through the years of silence. The bruises hidden beneath my clothes, the terror that had become my daily companion—all of it laid bare in front of her.

Mum's face hardened, her eyes narrowing into slits. "He's going, Lucy. He's not staying another day."

I nodded, numb and exhausted, but a flicker of hope ignited somewhere deep inside me. As Mum threw his clothes into black bin bags, she rang Dad, updating him.

"Lucy, are you alright?" Dad's voice trembled through the phone, heavy with guilt.

"I'm sorry, Dad. I didn't want you to find out. I'm so ashamed."

His voice cracked. "We knew something wasn't right, but we had no idea. I promise you; he'll pay for this. I thought it odd when he bought a knob-lock instead of a storage lock for that cupboard. When I questioned him about it, he blurted out some drivel about buying the wrong one and what did it matter. I could kill him."

I passed the phone back to Mum. "I need to save my strength for Jordan. Let's end this now."

Mum nodded; determination etched into her face. "We're going to his work."

Dad's voice came through the line again, "I've never been prouder of you girls."

We drove towards Birmingham in silence, my heart pounding with a mix of fear and adrenaline. Mum's calm steadied me as we pulled into the car park.

Charging past the receptionist, we went straight into the open-plan office.

"Hello, Lucy, long time no see," Ned, one of Jordan's colleagues, said as we approached. "Has Jordan forgotten his lunch?"

Lifting my chin, I pushed back my hair to reveal black and purple bruises across my left cheek and neck. "He's going to wish it was just his lunch. Where is he?"

"Went into a meeting ages ago, he's…"

Jordan appeared and on seeing me and Mum, he froze.

Mum scowled and dropped the bin bags on the floor. "Talk of the devil."

The room blurred until all I could see were Jordan's clenched fists. Suddenly scared, I cowered. Anger and fear blended until I didn't know which emotion was causing me to shake.

Jordan tried to play it cool in front of his colleagues, "Not now, Lucy. I'm busy. I'll ring you later."

I almost ran, but Mum's hand touched my elbow, it was all I needed. I stepped forward, my voice muted but dripping with venom. "You locked me in a wardrobe this morning and left me there. You know I'm terrified of the dark. Mum had to break the door down with your baseball bat."

Jordan's face turned beetroot red. "That's a lie!"

"Before you sink any further into lies, you should be aware that Mum set her phone to record while getting me out of the wardrobe as evidence for the police."

The room fell silent, all eyes on Jordan.

His bravado faltered. "Lucy, I'd never…"

Although my voice was quiet, strength and courage grew inside me. "You've been controlling me since the day we met.

But no more. That's why I'm here. I've finally seen the light. We're over. Don't come home."

His colleagues exchanged uneasy glances, some shaking their heads in disgust. His boss, Helen, stood up, her eyes blazing. "Jordan, conference room. Now."

Jordan's world crumbled around him as he walked away. Free at last, I'd never be his victim again. Relief came so hard that I started shaking uncontrollably. Mum wrapped her cardigan around me like a shield.

Michael jumped up and offered me his chair. In moments, his work colleagues who I thought detested me, rushed around all-consoling.

"Always knew he was a piece of shit," hissed Michael shaking his head. "Why on earth did you stay with him?"

I ignored that question; that deep, revealing answer would need addressing before I could ever talk to anyone about it.

"He told me you all hated me."

"It's so not true. Each time we saw you together we were worried about you. We couldn't say anything for fear of what Jordan might do."

I gave in to sobs, no longer embarrassed, just relieved.

Michael passed me a box of tissues. "Trust me, he'll never bother you again."

Dabbing at my face with a tissue, I nodded. It would be impossible for me to be a bigger mess but I glanced at Mum and smiled. I realised that my life was never going to be the same again.

I had been saved by Super-Mum and myself! Elated, I left the office punching the sky. The handcuffs were finally off.

If you would like to read the whole story, then please check out *Driven to Kill* a psychological thriller.

https://www.amazon.co.uk/Driven-Kill-Captivating-Psychological-Thriller-ebook/dp/B0DJFZFPGH

https://www.amazon.com/Driven-Kill-Captivating-Psychological-Thriller-ebook/dp/B0DJFZFPGH

Achilles Heel!

FRED AND LIVY lived three doors down from us, great friends and an integral part of our social scene. But of course, everything's changed now.

Livy and Jilly had their babies around the same time, spending countless hours in each other's houses sharing confidences, swapping baby stories, and putting the world to rights. This continued until Livy went back to work at the local primary school five years later. Livy always had a strong social conscience and was deeply involved in school and community activities as her kids grew up, keeping busy while Fred's job took him away every week and every other weekend. Neither of them seemed to mind the time apart—they were blissfully happy and excited for their twentieth wedding anniversary party.

The night before the celebration, I noticed Fred's car in their drive. Livy had made it clear he needed to be home early to help me with the marquee the next day while she and Jilly prepared the food. Jazz music would play through the night, and a bouncy assault course was set up for the teenagers and younger children. It was going to be a night to remember!

A few days later, Livy told me what happened later that night. Fred had arrived home utterly exhausted. After helping with a few preparations and a simple dinner, he went straight to bed, while Livy stayed up to finish a few chores. Fred would usually unpack as soon as he got back, a habit Livy appreciated—he was always tidy, with his wardrobe and drawers in immaculate order. She often admired the neatness while he was away, comparing it wistfully to the chaos left by their kids.

Feeling generous, Livy decided to spoil him. Although he might grumble, she opened his suitcase to unpack it, thinking she'd put any dirty laundry straight into the wash. But at the bottom of the suitcase, she found something strange: a photo of a woman, no more than thirty, holding a young boy's hand. As Livy looked closely, she recognized the child as Adam, one of her students, and the woman as Mrs Butler, who always dropped Adam off at school. Livy had even considered inviting Mrs Butler out for a drink sometime, assuming her husband was often away like Fred.

She thought perhaps Fred had picked up the wrong suitcase by mistake. But the clothes inside were undoubtedly his—she recognized his favourite shirts, which she'd bought to match his suits, and the old slippers he always took with him, his sentimental weakness: His Achilles Heel as I called them because he couldn't go anywhere without them. Confused and shaken, Livy had repacked the suitcase exactly as she'd found it.

The next morning, Jilly and I arrived early to start preparing for the party. Livy seemed unusually quiet, absorbed in phone calls and small tasks. Fred was unpacking his suitcase while glancing at the marquee instructions.

"Livy, are you alright? Let's have a coffee first," Jilly suggested.

Livy sighed. "There's so much to do, and I suppose I'm just panicking."

As we made drinks, Fred leaned in and murmured to me, "Livy's in a mood. I've no idea why, but it's probably best to steer clear."

"You've given her a card and a present, right?"

"Yes, but she barely looked at the card, she didn't even put the flowers in a vase—just left them in the sink! Normally, I'd get breakfast in bed..." Fred muttered, puzzled and shaking his head.

The morning passed quickly, and although there was an odd atmosphere, everything was ready by the time I went home to change for the party. When we arrived back, the marquee was beautiful, Livy was radiant in a peach dress, and Fred was nervously searching for his misplaced mobile.

Fred and Livy's kids were in charge of entertainment. Livy had asked them to include some extra family photos in the screen show they planned for later.

As the party got into full swing, we noticed Livy making several discreet calls, even rushing off to school to check something. Meanwhile, Fred grew frantic, unable to find his phone, looking more and more on edge. The kids' screen show was running in the background and we laughed as we saw our holiday photos of Cornwall show up. Our families had had some great holidays together; we hoped we would have plenty more.

The time for speeches arrived. As Fred spoke lovingly of their family, the kids, and the life they'd built, I saw Livy's eyes fill with tears. She turned away just as a woman and her young son entered the marquee. Livy walked over to them with a calm expression, guiding them towards Fred. The woman looked completely bewildered. When she saw Fred, her mouth fell open in shock. Fred froze.

With a steady hand, Livy offered Mrs Butler the framed photo she'd found. Fred glanced at Livy, and then buried his face in his hands, muttering, "I knew this day would come. I've dreaded it."

"What's going on?" Mrs Butler whispered, stunned. "Fred, why are you here with Adam's teacher? You told me you were in Finland!"

Before Mrs Butler could say another word, Fred grabbed Livy's hand, pulling her outside the marquee as everyone inside stood in silence, bewildered by the unfolding scene.

Their voices rose, breaking the silence. "Yes, I'm having an affair with Rona. Adam is my son. I never meant for it to happen… I love you and the kids, but I don't know how to escape this mess. How did you find out?"

"I saw the photo in your suitcase and started putting it all together," Livy replied, her voice breaking. "You've lied to me, to all of us. I teach her son for goodness sake! How could you, and how did you find the time?"

"I haven't been travelling, Livy. My job's been local. I've been staying with Rona…" Fred admitted, defeated.

"So that's why when I found letters with your name on them and a different address locally you said it was a post office box number!" said Livy.

"Yes," said Fred looking deflated.

People began to leave, leaving their gifts behind. Livy collapsed outside the marquee, comforted by her children, while

Fred returned to find Rona and Adam. I later heard that Rona had hurled her shoes at Fred in anger, with Adam sobbing as they climbed into a waiting Uber.

Within a week, Livy and Fred's house went up for sale. Livy, feeling betrayed and hurt, had thrown him out, and set about obtaining a divorce. Although Fred told Livy that Rona had known about her, Livy believed Rona's claim that she'd been as deceived as she was. The first thing he packed—his old slippers.

Jilly still sees Livy now and then. Livy recently mentioned that parents' evenings were surreal, with Fred trying to catch her eye or pass her notes. But she assured us she'd moved on. "I have someone now who respects me, someone I can trust and love." She laughed, "It's odd seeing Fred henpecked, with no sparkle, wearing suits and ties that look as worn and tired as he does. The kids tell me he keeps his old slippers boxed up for protection, his Achilles' heel, a reminder of all he's lost."

Santa's Revenge

Santa's dieting was making him blue,
People thought him too portly to fit down the flue.
Rudolph suggested a jog through the park,
Santa decided to *see him off* in the dark.

On delivery night, he tugged at his belt with a yell,
It's the sherry and mince pies! he started to dwell.
Try willpower, said Dancer, or give the treats a miss.
But the children want their gifts by the fire—they insist.

Parents will grumble if you get stuck and linger.
Fine, grumbled Santa, they can go to hell with my finger!
I'll drop the lot outside in a cluster,
If it snows, their gifts will weather and bluster.

On second thoughts, I'll rewrite Christmas, he roared,
No more mince pies, or sherry galore!
On Christmas Eve, I'll stay in and snore,
And let families shop till the stores close their doors!

The Twenty-Fourth Time

JILL WAS LATE, as usual. By the time she reached the Community Hub, a queue had already snaked its way out the door. *I'll be here for ages,* she thought, sighing as she resigned herself to missing her Pilates class. *If only I'd left on time instead of trying to do ten things at once!*

She pulled out her phone and tapped away, cancelling her class with a twinge of regret. "Damn those gym fines!" she muttered.

The bus delay hadn't helped, and it was bound to get worse—she was sure there'd be no custard creams left for her, only the dull, dry digestives she despised.

"Hi Jill! Twenty-fourth time today, isn't it?" called Edna, one of the volunteers.

"Yes, Edna," Jill replied with a tired smile. "It seems to come around faster every time. Just hoping I don't faint again."

Edna chuckled, trying to hold back a laugh. "Oh, yes, I remember last time. You fainted right outside—pouring rain, thunder, lightning, the works! We had to rush you in on a stretcher. By the time we got to you, you looked like a drowned rat!"

Jill stifled an embarrassed laugh and wondered if anyone could see the steam beginning to evaporate off her head. "Yes, I was soaked through. Though I did get a good lightning show. Could've been Bonfire Night with all those flashes and bangs!"

A flash memory of the teenagers jeering at her made her cheeks flare crimson.

Edna giggled, leaning in. "No toffee apples or hot dogs?"

"Not even a custard cream. Maybe today's my lucky day?" Jill joked, giving a hopeful smile.

"Oh, I'll make sure of it. Can't have you missing out on your favourites," Edna assured her with a wink.

"Thanks Edna, I can always rely on you."

With her patience wearing thinner than a pancake on a diet, Jill reached the front of the queue.

"Mrs Griffin, the nurse will see you now," called the clerk.

Jill lay down on the bed, watching a nurse in blue approach. "Right-handed or left-handed?" she asked briskly.

"Left," Jill answered, turning away as the needle approached.

"You won't feel a thing," the nurse promised. Always one to feel dizzy, Jill turned her head away and didn't look back until the nurse patted her arm with cotton wool when she'd finished. "Congratulations, Mrs Griffin. Next time, it'll be your twenty-fifth! You'll get a silver book and a certificate. Quite the prize!"

Jill smiled. "I'm looking forward to it."

"Head next door for tea and biscuits," the nurse continued. "I think Edna's saved you some custard creams." With a brief smile, she moved on to the next donor, Jill already a memory.

Jill savoured her tea and custard creams when the sound of a siren pierced the air.

Edna hurried over, looking shaken. "There's been a terrible accident on the M42. Twenty-four local children from St Peter's have been taken to hospital. I think your Ellie… and my granddaughter… might be among them."

Jill took Edna's hand as they stood in silent prayer, time hanging suspended around them.

Jill's phone pinged with new messages.

St Peter's: Please contact the school urgently.

NHS Text: All Blood Donations Count—give blood today and save someone's life…

The Watch

WHEN I ARRIVED at Mum's bungalow, I could tell she was excited. She stood waiting at the door, an unusual sight that only happened on special occasions or, heaven forbid, if I was late.

A glance at my watch assured me I was early. Phew!

She bustled me inside before I could take off my shoes and urged me to sit on the couch. "I have a surprise for you," she said, her eyes sparkling.

Curiosity piqued, I scanned the lounge for clues, but nothing seemed out of place. No matter. Mum's excitement was contagious, and after a few difficult months with her health, it was wonderful to see her so animated.

Flushed with delight, she disappeared into her bedroom and returned moments later with a small, long box. "Ta-dah!" she exclaimed, holding it out like a trophy.

My hands trembled as I took it. I shook the box playfully. "Is it a biro? One of those fancy ones from Monsoon?"

Mum laughed. "No, it isn't, and stop shaking it!"

Obediently, I lifted the lid. Inside, nestled in purple lining, was her beloved Gucci watch—an 18ct gold G-Timeless Multibee. Elegant and iconic, the watch radiated a bold simplicity that made it timeless. I had always loved it.

Mum had bought it years ago with inheritance money from her sister Attracta's estate. Attracta, her older sister, had meant the world to her. When dementia overtook Attracta, Mum had taken on the role of Power of Attorney, travelling to Ireland to oversee her care. The watch was more than a luxury—it symbolised their bond and the love they'd shared.

"I can't take this, Mum," I said, awed. "It means too much to you. It's a family heirloom now, and I always imagined you'd want to wear it for as long as you could. I know it reminds you of Attracta."

Her shoulders slumped like the broken wings of a bird. "But I want you to have it. I want to see you enjoying it."

Her enthusiasm softened my resistance, but I hesitated. "Have you checked with my sisters? It's worth a lot, and I wouldn't want them to feel left out."

Mum bristled. "Angela hasn't spoken to me in years. Neave is abroad and has plenty from me already. And Simone—well, she's had her share too. This is for you, my first gift to you."

Despite her insistence, I couldn't shake my caution. "Let's talk about it another day, Mum," I said, hugging her. "It's amazing that you've offered it to me. For now, how about that coffee you promised?"

The subject wasn't raised again until months later. Mum sat across from me, tears streaming down her face. "Simone says she wants the watch," she confessed. "She says it's unfair for me to give it to you."

My heart sank. "It's okay, Mum," I said, hugging her again. "I'll never forget the thought. Let's not let this upset us. It doesn't matter."

We moved on, sharing Mr Kipling's fancies and laughter, and the watch was tucked away once more.

The watch's story didn't end there. Mum's health and memory continued to decline. During our weekly shopping and catch-up visits, she would keep checking the gas hob and the door. She became very negative without a good word to say to anyone. The mum I knew was slipping away and it broke my heart. Diagnosed with early-onset dementia her slow decline had begun.

During one of our visits, she asked me to take the Gucci watch to Ireland, to Aida—Gavin's wife—who had been a lifeline for Attracta in her final years.

This time, I didn't ask questions. Mum had made her decision, and I respected it. Rob and I booked a trip to Ireland, and the watch made its journey to its new home.

Aida was stunned when I handed her the envelope. "My God! It's the Gucci watch. I wonder how your mum knew I would love it."

I took hold of Rob's hand for support. "Mum always knew you loved it and she wanted it to go to the family who helped and loved Attracta as much as she did."

Inside was a heartfelt letter from Mum.

> Dear Aida,
> I hope this finds you well. Please accept this watch as a token of my gratitude. It belongs to the family who loved and cared for Attracta as much as I did.
> I don't think I will be able to visit Ireland again as my health continues to decline, as does my memory. Please ensure Jill and Rob have a great weekend and introduce them to as many cousins as possible.

Take care,

Love, Patty

Aida's eyes glistened as she held the watch and read the letter over and over.

When we returned, Mum mentioned the visit to my sisters. Simone was furious, storming out of Mum's house. But by then, Mum's memory had grown fragile. She didn't recall the upset, only that the watch had found a good home.

Aida wears the watch to this day. Whenever she visited England, Mum would marvel at it, remarking how it reminded her of Attracta.

In the end, dementia took Mum just as it had her sister. To the end, we loved and took care of her and worked together to give her the best life possible.

The watch became a symbol of love and family, its journey a testament to the bonds that endure through time and memory.

It's a story I've never shared with my sisters. Some things, I believe, are best left as they are.

Something in the Cellar

THE DAY ANNA and Ron moved into their three-storey Victorian mews house in Dorridge, Anna felt like they had won the lottery. It was everything she had dreamed of: a grand home with servant bells in each room and a long, winding staircase that spiralled up through the centre of the house to the third floor. The sash windows were made of oak timber, with stained glass roses adorning the upper panes—a pattern that, as the saying went, 'grew on you.'

The oversized front door matched the windows, complete with its rose-themed panel, and even the garden seemed dedicated to the flower. Roses in every imaginable shade bloomed across the grounds. Moving in during spring had been a masterstroke; the garden looked like it belonged to a National Trust property. Anna had joked about selling tickets to the neighbours for a tour.

"How are we going to maintain this garden?" Anna asked Ron one day, half-serious, half-hopeful.

"That's your department, I'm afraid," he replied with a cheeky smile.

Ron was tall and slim, with brown hair and eyes, and a perpetually nerdy but happy demeanour. Anna sighed in exasperation, realising she'd indeed agreed to look after the garden. She couldn't believe he remembered—Ron usually forgot things like that.

The house held other surprises too. The cellar, when they found it, was lined with shelves and contained a large pump. It puzzled Anna. She prided herself on always reading the details of any property before signing contracts, but she hadn't noticed anything about a pump in the sales information.

"How did I miss that? I always read the small print," she asked Ron, annoyed at herself. Anna crossed her arms and tapped her foot. Her friends told her she was funny with a dry sense of humour—right now that was nowhere to be seen.

He grinned. "I don't know, my little blonde bombshell. I don't remember seeing anything about it either. It can't be used much, though."

Anna frowned. "It looks like the pump operates to drain water from the cellar. I have no idea where it goes. We should find out."

"I'll add it to the list," Ron said with a groan. "This house is exhausting!"

Anna put her head on his chest and he wrapped an arm around her. "Shall we go for a drink at our new local, The Railway and forget about all this for today."

"Yes!"

As spring turned into summer, Anna fell in love with the garden and quickly forgot about the cellar. The pump seemed to work fine, and the space was soon filled with wine, dry goods, and suitcases. She sometimes noticed a musty smell or heard the scurry of tiny feet, but growing up in the countryside had made her immune to the occasional rat or mouse. She simply locked the cellar door and got on with things.

A few months later, Anna and Ron were on holiday in Spain when they heard about severe storms hitting the UK. They briefly thought of home but trusted the sump pump system to handle any flooding. “It’s designed for this,” Anna said confidently, having read up on the system and understanding how it worked.

“Our trusty basement sump and pump system will remove groundwater from within the cellar, including any water that collects in the cavity's drain membranes.”

When they returned, the storms were still causing chaos. Roads were flooded, and flights were being diverted. At the airport, they had to navigate puddles to get on the bus that would take them to arrivals. By the time they reached home, they were exhausted and cold but glad to be back. Paul, their son, had kindly turned on the heating and left milk, bread, and beans for them. They settled in, enjoying the view of lightning through the sash windows, unaware of what awaited them.

The next morning, Ron went downstairs to make tea and immediately shouted, “Anna, come quickly!”

She rushed down to find water pooling across the wooden floor. “Oh blimey! What’s that smell?”

Ron was trying to open the cellar door, but as soon as he did, a torrent of water—and rats—burst into the hallway.

Using all their strength, they slammed the door shut again. Ron threw open the front door, and most of the rats darted outside, seemingly preferring the cold rain. Still, a few remained, scurrying through the house.

“We need to check for more rats,” Anna said, her voice shaking.

Ron nodded grimly. “Grab the traps from the kitchen.”

A large number of traps revealed the previous owner had the same problem.

As they placed the traps, Anna couldn't shake the feeling of being watched. She tucked her trousers into her socks and tried to ignore the scratching sounds all around them. Both she and Ron felt sick, their dream home now invaded.

Later, as the rain eased, they heard the pump struggling to keep up in the cellar.

"We need a second pump, and I don't care how expensive it is," Ron said. "This can't happen again."

Anna agreed, and after a call to Permagard, they arranged for an engineer to assess the damage.

The engineer, Sid, arrived within hours. Tall and freckled, with sandy brown hair, he got straight to work. He inspected the cellar, noting the reduced water level, and suggested leaving a dehumidifier until a dual pump system could be installed the following week. They accepted his reasonable quote and arranged the date for his return to install the new dual pump system.

After Anna and Ron walked Sid out, they were attacked by two squirrels that seemed to come out of nowhere. The creatures bit and scratched, forcing the stunned Anna and Ron to fend them off with brooms and a grabber. When a trail of peanuts to an outside tree failed to lure the squirrels away, they called the Wildlife Protection Service.

The officers arrived like a scene from Ghostbusters and after thirty minutes of hoo-ha they capture the squirrels. Like knights in shining armour, they wash Anna and Ron's wounds and leave them a supply of antiseptic cream before leaving.

Exhausted, Anna sank onto the sofa with Ron. "Squirrels attacking us in Dorridge," she muttered. "Who would have thought it?"

Passing the Problem

I'D HEARD ABOUT the car park and its perfidious change of use, but I didn't think much of it at the time. A car park is a car park, right? But when *it* happened, it was a different story altogether.

One day, the car park was suddenly covered with rubble. Not a few bricks here and there—oh no, we're talking about a proper mountain of the stuff. It was as if a demolition site had relocated overnight. Needless to say, parking there was now as likely as me winning the lottery without buying a ticket.

Ordinarily, I might have raised an objection. But it was unregistered land, and the place had become a hotbed for drug dealers. Adults and school kids alike were treating it as their one-stop shop for illegal highs, and frankly, I didn't think that was reasonable—especially for the kids. I suppose my attitude boiled down to, "As long as it's not happening on my doorstep, someone else can deal with it." I wanted to move the problem to another area, hoping local children would stop buying drugs and the village would return to a quiet, sleepy hollow again. Selfless, I know.

When the rubble arrived, the village threw a bit of a celebration. "This'll sort them out!" people cheered. The drug dealers were going to have to find a new postcode, and we all hoped it wouldn't be ours. That evening, Ron and I went to the local for a celebratory drink, and when we came home at ten, the neighbourhood was blissfully quiet.

"It's lovely and peaceful again," I said, brimming with optimism. "I don't know where those drug dealers will go now."

"Don't count your chickens," Ron muttered, tapping his nose like a budget Mystic Meg. "This won't end well."

The next morning, my phone pinged with a text from one of the neighbours—a very panicked one at that. She'd come home late the previous night in a taxi, only to spot a dodgy van lurking in the turning circle near our houses. Apparently, there were two blokes inside, smoking something that definitely wasn't Marlboro Lights. She said they were acting shiftily and thought they might be selling drugs.

Naturally, this put the whole neighbourhood on red alert. It had taken years to get rid of the dealers at the old car park, and the last thing we wanted was for them to set up shop right outside our homes. The turning circle was already a nightmare in the dark; now it had potential as the new HQ for our friendly neighbourhood criminals.

We gathered outside later that day to discuss our plan of action.

"As a temporary measure, we'll put up a chain and a padlock across the entrance," suggested one of the neighbours. "And maybe a sign saying there's CCTV in operation."

"We can decide on the camera location once we've agreed where to install it," added the woman who'd seen the van.

The plan sounded solid, and everyone pitched in. I called the council and the police for advice, though neither was particularly helpful. Apparently, because we live on a private road, the police could do little unless the dealers were caught red-handed. Fat lot of good that was.

The chain and padlock went up that very evening, and for two weeks, it became a nightly ritual—lock up at dusk, unlock at dawn. It felt like we were running some sort of exclusive gated community, but instead of keeping out the riff-raff, we were keeping out actual criminals.

Eventually, the CCTV camera was installed, complete with a shiny new sign warning potential troublemakers. And, just like that, the two drug dealers disappeared. Vanished into thin air. The neighbourhood was safe again—at least for now.

We patted ourselves on the back and threw a little celebration, though I couldn't help but think about the bigger picture. The problem hadn't been solved; it had just been shifted a few miles down the road. Some other poor council would have to deal with it now.

"Let's raise a toast," I said at the party, holding up my glass. "To peace and quiet—for us, anyway."

I couldn't shake the irony. While we celebrated our victory, someone else was waking up to the exact same nightmare. But hey, at least our turning circle was safe. Small wins, eh?

An Episode Remembered

LOOKING BACK AT my childhood, one memory always stands out: the day Dad brought home a Post Office van for the family.

Mum's reaction was immediate, and it wasn't exactly joy. "Doug, have you completely lost your marbles? That van won't hold us all, and it's far too distinctive. What will the neighbours think? I refuse to set foot in it."

Dad, ever the optimist, brushed her off with a grin. "Come on, Pam, it's not so bad. The garage across the road will re-spray it pale blue. You won't even remember it was a Post Office van."

"What do you think, kids?" he asked, looking to us for backup.

Simone, the eldest, jumped in immediately. "I think it's cool!"

"I love it!" I chimed in, adjusting my blue glasses with a serious air. "As long as I don't have to wear that horrid yellow raincoat and sou'wester hat in it. You know I hate them." I stamped my foot for emphasis.

Mum's mouth twitched as though she was trying not to laugh. "Alright, I didn't know you hated it that much."

"You must remember," I pressed on, "the bus driver shouted, 'Where's the pot of gold?' in front of everyone. Mortifying!"

Dad scratched his head. "But it keeps you dry, doesn't it? Kay's always had good taste, and she passed it down to you!"

"Not this time, Dad. The labels were still attached, which means even Kay refused to wear it," I said, turning on the waterworks for good measure.

Dad gave in first. "She's right, Pam. She shouldn't have to wear it. I'll take her to Birmingham for a new coat."

"Thanks, Dad! You're the best!" I made a beeline for the bin with the offending coat and hat.

Mum wasn't done yet, though. "Doug, where's the money for the coat coming from? You've spent it all on that heap of junk. That little minx has twisted you around her little finger again!"

"Pam," Dad said, putting on his most charming tone and ignoring the last question, "come and sit in the van. Get a feel for it. A second-class ride is better than a first-class walk, eh?"

He started massaging her neck, and soon she melted. "Alright, let's see the heap of junk, then."

We all charged outside to see the van. There it stood, a vivid red, its Post Office past obvious to anyone with eyes.

"You'd better get it painted straight away," Mum warned.

"It's going to the garage this afternoon," Dad assured her. "Ron's doing it as a favour. And tomorrow, I'm getting some seats from the Midland Red buses—plush, red leather ones. You'll love them!"

"What about windows?" Mum asked, arms crossed.

"Ah, trickier," Dad admitted. "We'll get them eventually. For now, it'll do. At least I can get to work, and we'll have something to replace the Triumph Herald. Insurance pay-out should come soon."

"It all makes sense. Hopefully, the insurance will pay out fairly soon, and we can buy something better for the family. Sorry for being so negative."

Dad looked hopeful, and I didn't understand why. Dad had been friends with Ron for years and even went to his son John's wedding. Dad had also designed their office and spent many happy hours there smoking and catching up with his friend.

The next evening, the van returned resplendent in pale blue. Ron had done a brilliant job with the paint and fitted the bus seats perfectly—well, almost perfectly.

Dad, thrilled with himself, invited us all for a spin. We clambered into the back, jostling for the best seats, while Mum climbed into the front, looking surprisingly glamorous with her handbag perched on her lap.

Dad, shouted at us to calm down and then we were off to Hinckley, to Uncle Danny's and Aunty Mary's to show them our new purchase.

As the car moved into first gear, we all cheered, and although we couldn't see where we were going, we were hyper.

"Be quiet back there," shouted Mum, although we could tell she was happy.

"Here's to the open road!" Dad announced, pulling away.

We hadn't even gone a mile before chaos erupted in the back. The seats, unbolted and unsecured, started sliding and crashing into each other.

Suddenly, we turned a corner, and the seats in the back started to move and ended up crashing into each other.

"Ow! My foot!" Simone yelled.

"I can't find my shoe!" Ian wailed, his voice trembling. Right then, I remembered how terrified of the dark he was!

"Doug, stop the van!" Mum shouted, her tone leaving no room for argument.

Dad pulled over, sweating profusely. Mum stormed out, flung open the back doors, and began pulling Ian out, murmuring soothingly while shooting daggers at Dad.

"There, there, darling, Mummy's here."

"My foot hurts," cried Simone.

"Is it red?"

"No, but it hurts."

"Let me make sure Ian's okay."

"Okay, Mum."

"Doug, get back here now."

"Yes darling, coming straight there."

Ian whimpered, "I was scared and couldn't see where we were going. Everything started moving. I hurt Simone, I think, but I didn't mean to."

Simone upped the level of crying to wailing, "It's all your fault!"

"Mum, tell her I didn't mean to. I couldn't see what was happening. I was thrown all over the place."

“Shut up the lot of you. Doug! Where are you?”

Ian chortles, “I think Dad is running away. He’s in the distance but keeps looking behind.”

“He’d better be going to your Uncle Danny’s! Simone, let’s look at your foot.”

Danny arrived not long after, Dad riding in the passenger seat of his car, sheepish but waving a white handkerchief like a flag of surrender. I got the giggles.

Going straight over to Mum, Danny said, “Hi, Pam. I hear Doug has got himself in a bit of trouble.”

Mum raised her eyes heavenwards.

“Doug, what on earth have you done?” Uncle Danny asked, chuckling.

“He’s put the kids’ lives in danger, that’s what!” Mum snapped. “Who in their right mind installs seats in the back of a van without bolts? Maybe an Irish fool cursed by the Blarney Stone!”

Uncle Danny burst out laughing. “I told him years ago to leave that stone alone!”

Even Mum couldn’t hold back her laughter at that, and Dad, sensing his moment, dropped the handkerchief and joined us by the van.

It took weeks to fix the van properly, but it became a family legend, often retold at gatherings—especially by Dad, who always added, “A second-class ride really is better than a first-class walk… as long as the seats stay put!”

Someone I Knew

THERE'S MUCH TO be said for Karma. But let's be honest—it's not always fair.

I worked with Jackie for six years in the 1990s, back in Leicester. She was fun, loud, and always had sparkling brown eyes and a wicked smile. Jackie was our CEO's PA, effortlessly elegant with her long black hair and the most tanned legs I'd ever seen. She wasn't a size eight – a bit fuller – but, my God, she was mesmerising. Jackie had a daughter, Laura, who was practically her twin but smaller.

Her boyfriend, Pete, was a rent collector in the Borough. Pete was the definition of happy-go-lucky, with a head full of curly blond hair. He and Jackie were always jetting off somewhere exotic, their tans growing darker with every return. Jackie would slather on any oil she could find, and she always looked sensational, like she belonged in a travel magazine.

Jackie's office had a revolving door of admirers. People would pop in under any flimsy pretext, just to gawp at her beauty. I was one of them. My name's David, and I'll admit it: I was in awe of her. Pete was the cat that got the cream, and he knew it.

"I'm riding the wave and enjoying every minute," Pete would say whenever someone teased him about his luck. "There's more to Jackie than just good looks. Otherwise, I'd be out of here."

I worked in rent and rebates back then, a gangly nineteen-year-old with jet-black hair and not a single ounce of confidence. Jackie was at least twenty-five years older than me, but I still couldn't help staring. She was Leicester's answer to Sophia Loren.

Fast Forward Twenty Years

Driving down from London, the back seats were a battlefield. My daughters, Alexa and Pippa, weren't fist fighting yet, but they were working up to it. Claire, my wife, sat in the passenger seat with her headphones on, blissfully unaware of the chaos. She gave my hand a squeeze and smiled. I smiled back—a futile attempt to pretend everything was fine.

Giving up, I know I will have to control the mayhem behind the front seats or put up with the consequences. "Girls! Keep the noise down! We're only fifteen minutes away from Nan and Granddad's."

That got their attention. I could practically see the pound signs in their eyes as they called a truce.

"Okay, Daddy," Alexa chirped. "We'll be good, won't we, Pippa?"

Pippa nodded so hard in the rear-view mirror that I thought her head might fall off.

At Nan and Granddad's, it was the usual welcome: hugs, tea, and poker. My parents had made the grave mistake of teaching Alexa and Pippa to play cards for cash, and the girls were merciless.

"Get the cards out, Granddad," Alexa announced. "I feel a winning streak coming on."

Granddad grinned like a man walking to his doom. Meanwhile, Pippa buttered up Grandma with compliments about her hair, which earned her extra biscuits.

"Why, thank you, love. I had it done this morning." Grandma patted her curly grey locks.

"Mum," I said, pulling Claire towards the door. "We need to head off straight away. I'm dropping Claire at her mum's, and then I'm going into Leicester. Jackie's retiring, and I've been invited to her leaving do."

"Oh, that'll be lovely! Say hello to Jackie for me," Mum said, waving us off.

"Kids, be good for your grandparents. See you later."

"Can I get anything for you from the shops?" asked Claire, looking at her watch.

"Thanks, Claire, but no, we have everything we need. Say Hello to Beryl from us."

"Will do."

Back on the road, I gave Claire a smile, "That went well, lovely to see Mum and Dad. Hope the kids treat them well today."

"Well, you know them as well as I do. I did speak to them before we left, but Alexa is growing up and is a teenager, it could be difficult," said Claire as she started picking at her hands.

"I know you try with her, don't get upset."

"It's so difficult now, especially with Pippa understanding what's happening."

Looking Claire straight in the eyes as we wait by the traffic lights, I say quietly, "It makes it so much harder to bear for all of us, especially you."

Claire puts on a bright face, "Anyway, here we are."

"I'll pop in and say hello to Beryl and then leave you girls to wander the shops for a few hours."

"Have a great leaving do for Jackie. Say hello to the gang for me. Don't mention our problems to Mum you know how she worries."

I put my hand in front of my mouth and do the 'zip' action.

Jackie's Leaving Do

As I parked outside the council offices, I noticed how small the place seemed now. Built in the 1950s, it was a depressing combination of grey walls and blue windows, but back in the day, it had felt enormous.

I walked in with a bouquet of flowers for Jackie, eager to see her glamorous self again. The canteen buzzed with laughter – no change there – and I spotted a sea of older, greyer versions of my former colleagues. In the centre of it all was Pete, still holding court. But then I saw her.

Her hair was still jet-black, though clearly dyed, and her heels were as skyscraper-high as ever. But time had left its mark. Her once-smooth skin sagged slightly, and her twinkling eyes looked tired. Still, there was no mistaking her.

"You're late, as usual!" she said, pulling me into a hug that smelled faintly of Chanel No. 5 and nostalgia.

"You know me only too well."

The new CEO's speech was the usual fare—full of platitudes and clichés. Jackie wiped away a tear as Pete held her hand. When it was her turn to speak, she rose shakily, clutching a glass of wine like it was a lifeline.

"Thank you all for thirty wonderful years," she said, her voice trembling. "I'll miss you all – even Pete!" Everyone laughed, and she grinned. "For my next job, I'll be volunteering as a grandma. My daughter, Laura, is in hospital as we speak, having her first baby."

Finally, it's time for the buffet, and I understand how carefree my life was back in the day. How I long for those days now.

I caught up with old friends, showed them pictures of Claire and the kids, and laughed about the good old days. But as I watched Jackie, now a grandmother-to-be, I couldn't shake a pang of envy. Her life seemed perfect, while mine felt like it was falling apart. Where did we go wrong?

After saying goodbye, I left the party and arrived at Beryl's thirty minutes later, just as they arrived back from shopping.

I wave to Beryl and Claire gets in the car.

"Did you have a good time, darling?"

Her face was a reflection of sadness. "It was perfect until I broke down in tears, and Mum wormed it out of me. She offered to come up and stay next week to give us both a rest. Sorry, it's difficult to be cool, calm and collected for several hours."

"Don't worry, love. Hopefully, all will have gone well, and we can head home after dinner."

“Do you want to see what I brought?”

“Wait till we arrive at Mum and Dad’s when I’m not driving. I’m sure whatever you have brought will be fabulous.”

Claire puts in her earphones and taps the dashboard. It was not long until I recognised the tune and started singing along… “All is well in our world...”

We drive into my parent’s road, we stop holding hands, and I feel on top of the world.

The Crisis

As soon as we pulled into the drive, the scene was chaos. Mum met us at the door, pale and shaking.

“Alexa’s upstairs,” she said. “It’s bad, David. She’s… she’s hurt herself. Pippa wouldn’t let us ring you.”

Feared gripped my chest like a vice.

Claire was out of the car and inside the house before I could even process the words. I followed a few seconds later, heart pounding, to find Alexa on the floor, sobbing in Claire’s arms. Her arms were bound, her mouth bloodied. She’d sewn it shut.

“What happened?” I demanded with sudden pains making me clutch my chest.

Mum explained through tears that a poker game had gone wrong. Alexa had tipped the table and run upstairs. Pippa had tried to warn them, but by then it was too late.

“We called an ambulance,” Dad said, his voice breaking. “They’re waiting for your decision.”

I caught Dad's eye and saw the pain in them. We hadn't told them and just assumed all would be well. "Dad, are you okay?"

Shaking, "I'll be fine. Not sure about Alexa. We called an ambulance as soon as we saw what she'd done to herself."

Pippa hugged her knees and sobbed. "I tried to stop it. I ran after her, but I was too late."

I pull her up and into my arms, kissing her head and holding her tight. "It's not your fault, Pippa."

A Family Torn

The paramedics arrived, and as they carried Alexa out, she spat venomous words at us. "You could've looked after me at home!" she screamed. "You bastards!"

Claire broke down, her composure shattered. "We're doing this because we love you," she whispered.

"You made the right decision, we'll look after her," said the paramedic called John.

As the ambulance drove away, the silence in the house was deafening. I held Pippa close, her sobs shaking us both. Claire stood by the window, staring out at nothing.

"Did we make the right decision?" I asked her later, my voice barely audible. She didn't answer. She didn't have to.

The drive home was quiet, except for the faint hum of Claire's relaxation tape. I reached for her hand, and she squeezed mine tightly. Life might not be fair, but for now, we were holding on.

Somebody's Hobby

MY NAME IS BRIAN, and I can't wait for the weekend when Eric is hosting a party at his house. It's the highlight of the year. I've finally made it—I even have a proper embossed invite.

Eric is my new best friend; we're as different as chalk and cheese. He's from a rich family, tall, very good-looking, slim but athletic, with short black hair, big brown eyes, and a wicked sense of humour. He's a sharp dresser who always wears the best of everything, especially the coveted Nike 270s. I, on the other hand, am five foot ten, slightly chubby, with blond hair and hazel eyes. I always wear jeans and an AC/DC T-shirt from the local market stalls. You can tell I'm from a poorer background—I work two jobs while studying at college. No matter what I do, I can't afford high-end shoes. Instead, I wear Primark's finest!

When I get to Eric's, the party is in full swing. Everyone who's anyone is already here, wearing their latest trainers. Eric is propping up the bar as usual and waves me over. I notice his trainers are more traditional tonight—black and white—which is unusual for him. They're classy, and I'm immediately drawn to them. He must own a pair of every trainer ever made; his wardrobe must be enormous.

Right then, I decide I would no doubt be more popular with the girls if I dressed like Eric. I briefly admire the sleek design and cushioning of his trainers, thinking that with shoes like these on my feet, I'd have more fun, enjoy dancing, and maybe even impress Grace. She's the local blonde heartthrob sitting in the corner, showing off her high-end trainers, slim figure, and knee-length navy dress. Her hair is tied back in a ponytail—she can't be more than five foot six, with big hazel eyes and the widest smile you've ever seen. The lads hover around her, practically drooling over her and her shoes. I'm not entirely sure what they all see in her.

By the time it gets to midnight, Eric is looking worse for wear. His words are slurring, and he stumbles into Grace.

I'm relatively sober in comparison, so I move to help him off her. Grace gives me a quick smile before glancing down at my feet in disgust. She wags her finger at me, and I hurry to pull Eric away.

Eric apologises and staggers off to his bedroom for a lie-down. I'm worried about him, so I open his bedroom door and follow him inside. His palatial room looks like something straight out of Country Life or Vogue. I've never had the luxury of reading either magazine, but this is the best bedroom I've ever seen. Eric is sprawled out on a rug near his bed, so I somehow manage to lift him onto it.

"Thanks, Brian, I love you," he mumbles.

"I'll get you undressed. Get some sleep, and I'll see you in the morning."

I pull off his trainers, admiring the smooth texture and construction of the shoes. They're my size! Without a second thought, I slip them on. They feel incredible, and I decide then and there to keep them.

Before leaving, I can't resist opening his wardrobe. It's like reaching Mecca. Every shoe is proudly displayed, cleaned to within an inch of its life, and waiting to be picked for that special occasion.

An adrenaline rush courses through me as I head for the door, where Grace is waiting outside.

"Did you get them, Brian?" she asks.

"Of course. When have I ever let you down?"

"There's always a first time."

"Not today. I love the thrill of the chase, and I get to wear his trainers, at least for tonight."

"We'll add them to the collection, then. He'll be too drunk to notice, and Daddy will buy him a new pair."

"Let's make use of the guest bedroom, then," I say, exhilaration pulsing through me.

"Don't be an idiot. Incest is not a good look, even for you."

"Spoilsport."

I know I could have done anything dark and wicked with Eric tonight; nothing is off-limits in my twisted mind. But I refrain. Grace—my sister—is my wingman, and these trainers are destined to join my growing collection.

Who Says Farewell?

From the editor...

So here we are, at the book's very end,
With tales of drama, where worlds twist and bend.
From shifts at work to a Facebook scroll,
Each story has spark, heart, and soul.

We've met Rob at football, in whirlwind romance,
And solved some problems (with half a chance).
Through laughs and twists, a surprise or two,
Jill's wit and charm have shone right through.

"Who says?" you ask. Well, Jill has the say,
With words that brighten each cloudy day.
She's travelled the world, her stories abound,
In humour and heart, her treasures are found.

So raise a glass (or a mug of tea),
Here's to Jill's tales, as rich as can be.
Though this is the end, the smiles will last,
A fond farewell to this wonderful cast!

Thank you for reading my collection of short stories, I hope you enjoyed them. If you have a moment to leave me a review on Amazon or Goodreads I would appreciate it.

Thanks again.

Jill

If you enjoyed Who Says, you might like my other collection of short stories.

https://www.amazon.com/Telling-Tales-Jill-Griffin-ebook/dp/B09N9X9LT6

https://www.amazon.co.uk/Telling-Tales-Jill-Griffin-ebook/dp/B09N9X9LT6

If you would like to find out what happens to Lucy after reading 'Living the Dream' and 'Can I See,' then you might want to check out *Driven to Kill:*

https://www.amazon.com/Driven-Kill-Captivating-Psychological-Thriller-ebook/dp/B0DJFZFPGH

https://www.amazon.co.uk/Driven-Kill-Captivating-Psychological-Thriller-ebook/dp/B0DJFZFPGH

> *"Driven to Kill had me hooked from the very first page and I found myself completely absorbed. Lucy's journey is so intense, and I kept questioning everyone's motives along with her, which made it hard to put down. Just when I thought I had everything figured out, another twist would completely throw me off.*
>
> *The characters felt so real, and the emotional tension made it much more than just a typical thriller for me and by the end, I was still thinking about the choices Lucy had to make. If you love thrillers with complex characters and a plot that keeps you guessing right up to the last page, Driven to Kill is definitely worth the read."* – Amazon US Review

Printed in Great Britain
by Amazon

52764057R00096